TORN'S LAW

Mary's hands were clasped tightly in her lap. They parted, and she held one out, palm up. The derringer was in it. Torn now had the leisure to identify the weapon as a double-barreled .22 caliber Frank Wesson with ivory grips.

"I believe this is what you're looking for," she said.

He made no move to confiscate the gun.

"Perhaps you should hold onto it for a while."

"The thought did cross my mind."

"Are you acquainted with firearms, ma'am?"

"I can manage, thank you. But go ahead and take it. It doesn't belong to me. Unlike my husband, I'm not one to take what isn't mine. It belongs to the gentleman you just ... um ... removed."

Torn said, "Some say that possession is nine points of the law."

HANK EDWARDS

THE JUDGE

Harper Paperbacks

Harper & Row, Publishers, New York
Grand Rapids, Philadelphia, St. Louis, San Francisco
London, Singapore, Sydney, Tokyo, Toronto

Harper Paperbacks a division of Harper & Row, Publishers, Inc.
10 East 53rd Street, New York, N.Y., 10022

Cover illustration by Darrell Sweet

First printing: October, 1990

Printed in the United States of America

HARPER PAPERBACKS and colophon are trademarks of Harper & Row, Publishers, Inc.

10 9 8 7 6 5 4 3 2 1

THE
JUDGE

CHAPTER 1

"EXCUSE ME, MA'AM. ARE YOU IN SOME KIND OF trouble?"

Mary Dobson hadn't heard the man come up behind her. She was standing at the very edge of the depot platform, straining her ears to catch the first sound of the train that she prayed was on its way. Her eyes were fastened to the flat and featureless eastern horizon, at the point where the arrow-straight track—and the telegraph line that accompanied it—dwindled in the prairie distance.

The man walked softly. The warped and weathered planking scarcely creaked beneath his tread. What little noise he made just didn't register with Mary Dobson, so intent was her concentration on that far point where, if it came at all, her salvation would first appear.

Turning, she forced a smile.

"No, of course not." By now she was so used to flying

1

false colors that it came naturally to her. "Why do you ask?"

He was tall, taller than most, and on the lanky side. His wheat-colored hair was close-cropped. His face was clean-shaven, and brown cheeks were pulled over strong bones. The mouth was wide, the lips thin. The eyes were steel-cast gray. There was something melancholy and grim about him. Those eyes had seen much hardship; the hard set of the mouth had seldom been eased by a smile.

"I beg your pardon, ma'am," he said, with the trace of a southern drawl. "I don't mean to pry. But in my line of work, most people I deal with are in trouble. After a while it becomes right easy to see it in a person."

Mary gave him a long look. Could she trust this man? Was there anybody in the entire state of Kansas that she *could* trust?

"And what kind of work do you do?"

"I'm a federal judge, ma'am. Clayton Torn, at your service."

He touched the brim of his hat, noticing that her dark eyes, pools of liquid hazel above prominent cheekbones, held a murky glimmer of fear.

It occurred to her that he was dressed rather like a judge. He seemed stern and austere in his dusty black frock coat, plain white muslin shirt closed at the collar with a string tie, black trousers and scuffed, spurless black boots. He wasn't wearing a gun. At least she didn't see one; he didn't have a shellbelt strapped on.

He had honest eyes. She needed someone to confide in. She was alone and lonely. But Mary cautioned herself. She didn't dare trust this man. Especially if he was a judge. Her husband was a very powerful man. Ike Dobson bought judges the same way he bought livestock.

"Thank you for your concern," she said with stiff formality. "But I'm not in any trouble, Mr. Torn. So I have no need of your assistance."

She turned away to resume her vigil.

It was an open-and-shut case of dismissal. Still, Torn hesitated. He knew she was lying. She *was* in trouble. He wanted to help. But he was too much the gentleman to force her to accept his help.

He went back to the bench, sat down next to his belongings, a black leather hand valise and a plain saddle. A Winchester 44/40 repeating rifle rode in the saddle boot.

The bench stood in a ribbon of precious shade cast by the Pitchfork Slough depot. The depot itself had once been a boxcar, part and parcel of the Atchison, Topeka & Santa Fe Railroad's inventory of rolling stock. It had been pulled off its trucks and onto a beam foundation to serve in its new function. This had been a simpler matter than building a structure; to find decent timber in sufficient quantity out here on the tallgrass prairie was no small feat.

Eyes narrowed against the glare of the summer sun, Clay Torn scanned his surroundings. There wasn't much to the town of Pitchfork Slough. A half-dozen dugouts and sod houses. A clutter of outbuildings: a smoke house, a couple of hog pens and cow sheds, several privies. All located north of and behind the boxcar-depot.

He had arrived late yesterday and had boarded at a railside tavern of sorts. A leather-skinned widow woman had added a room to her soddy, and put up a sign. She quenched the thirst of iron road passengers with bad whiskey while the trains took on water.

All in all, Pitchfork Slough was a squalid place, dozing now in the sweltering heat of mid-afternoon. Torn was past ready to put it behind him.

The station agent came out to lean in the doorway of the boxcar-depot. A hot, dry Kansas wind shredded the curlicues of aromatic smoke lifting from the bowl of his pipe.

"Saw you talking to the lady. Looks to me like she's wound up tighter than an eight-day clock."

His name was Schuyler. He was an old codger by frontier standards. Past fifty, short, and no heavier than the young woman he spoke about, but straight and spry. He wore a calico shirt with rolled up sleeves, suspendered corduroy pants tucked into mule-ear boots. His beard was gray bristle. There was a thick sheen of perspiration on his bald head.

Torn said nothing. He was not one for idle conversation. Schuyler, though, was determined to strike up a parley.

"Don't look like you had any better luck than I did. When she rode in this morning and bought that one-way to Wichita, I tried my utmost. That was 'fore you come over from the widder woman's. But she'd have none of it. Just commenced to standing over yonder. Watching for the train."

Torn looked at the woman. Her raven hair was done up beneath a flat-brimmed hat. The hatstring was pulled tight under the smooth strong curve of her jawbone. A well-tailored serge traveling outfit bespoke of money, and complimented her trim-waisted figure. High leather riding boots were hand-tooled. A lady of substance, mused Torn. There was Indian blood in her; that dusky complexion was not entirely due to long exposure to western sun and wind.

"Now, don't get me wrong," said Schuyler, undeterred by Torn's silence. "Out here, it's a wise man who minds his own business. But I feel sorry for her. She's got troubles. That's as clear as mother's milk."

Torn thought, *if a person could will a thing into happening, then for certain she'd will that westbound across all those long, empty miles of iron rail and right up alongside this depot.*

Schuyler carried on. "When I asked if my pipe smoke bothered her she gave me a strange look, and smiled kinda sad. Said that it didn't. That it reminded her of her grandfather. Reckon he smokes a pipe. Also reckon he's the one she's running back to."

"You think she's running?"

"Don't you? There're some clues point to it. The condition of that fine thoroughbred she rode in on, for one. She done melted that blue-blood's tallow. Any other horse and I reckon she'd be walking right this minute. And more than a hatful of miles shy of here. Then, when she bought the ticket, I asked her what I was supposed to do with it. The horse, I mean. She said someone would be along shortly to take care of it."

Torn nodded. Walking over from the widow's soddy, he had seen the handsome sorrel tied up behind the boxcar-depot. A fine, strong-looking animal, ridden hard. Schuyler was right. She was lucky to have reached Pitchfork Slough mounted.

He hadn't been as lucky. His horse had broken a foreleg in a prairie dog hole. Torn had put it down for good with a bullet in the brainpan. Then, toting his saddle and valise, he had walked the last ten miles to Pitchfork Slough.

"There's something else," added Schuyler. "You notice the way she keeps throwing looks over her shoulder, checking her backtrail? Something—somebody—is after her."

Torn had seen this. He knew what it was like to be hunted, and could sympathize with the woman.

She turned sharply and came over to them.

Torn stood up, removed his hat. It was an unconscious gesture that interested Schuyler. Clay Torn was plainly a gentleman of breeding. Eastern-born, reckoned the agent, but for certain a man forged in the west. As tough a customer as any hardcase who ever cut teeth on a gun barrel. Yet, still a man who minded his manners in the presence of a lady.

Mary Dobson barely spared Torn a glance.

"I've got to catch that train," she told Schuyler.

Her tone was intense, her voice ragged. Both men were shocked, and quite a bit embarrassed, to see her thin veneer of calm composure crumbling like old adobe. Tears gleamed in her desperate eyes. That delicately curved upper lip trembled slightly.

"It'll come," promised Schuyler. "Just give her time."

"I'm out of time. If it doesn't come, and soon, I'm as good as dead."

CHAPTER 2

"THE STATION DOWN-LINE SENT THE SIGNAL OVER
an hour ago," explained Schuyler. "She's running behind
schedule. But just hold tight, ma'am. Won't be long you'll
see her smoke."

She looked over her shoulder, back down the line, at
that far point where the earth touched the hem of the sun-
bleached sky. Torn looked, too, hoping for her sake to
see the smoke from the locomotive's diamond stack. But
there wasn't any smoke to see.

For an uncomfortable moment, no one spoke. The relentless prairie wind tugged at their clothes, then swept
past to ripple the limitless sea of grass. Above them, the
OK windmill was racketing at high speed.

"I can't afford to miss that train," she whispered.

Schuyler glanced over at the pale, freckle-faced, sandy-
haired boy who for the past couple of hours had been
walking the rails near the platform, arms outstretched like

7

those of a circus tightrope artist as he fought the wind to keep his balance. Torn guessed that he was thirteen or fourteen years old. A shy boy on the brink of manhood, and fascinated by the young woman, but too bashful to stare at such a vision of loveliness. The railwalking was his way of trying to draw her attention.

"Hey, Case!" called the agent. "Take her pulse for me, son."

The boy waved, and lay down to press his lank frame against one of the rails, putting ear to iron. Mary Dobson watched anxiously.

"My son," said Schuyler, a father's pride strong in his voice. "Named him after General John Casement. I worked with the general laying the U.P. main line. Was a brakey on the boarding train."

"Don't feel nothin', Pa," hollered Case.

Mary Dobson winced.

"It'll come," Schuyler assured her. "Got some crank boiling on the potbelly. Why don't you two come inside and have some?"

"You're very kind," said Mary, "but, for myself, no. Thank you."

Torn admired her for her courtesy. It had to be difficult for her, in the state she was in, to even think about civility.

"Don't get much in the way of company out here. It's a lonesome spot. Hundred miles from nowhere. The folks living back behind here are Dutch, or some such. They ain't long on talk. Just as well, 'cause I can't understand none of that foreign lingo anyway. Nearest real town is Cottonwood Falls. A good day's ride. All else in between is prairie. Part of a big ranch. Ike Dobson's ranch."

He cut his eyes at her, speculatively, as he uttered the name. She had given the name Mary Chubb for the passenger list he would provide the westbound's conductor.

But if there was trouble in this part of Kansas, odds were that Ike Dobson had something to do with it.

But Mary wasn't paying any attention to Schuyler. Instead, she was watching the boy, who now sat on the slope on the track siding in the black shade cast by the water tower. The boy was staring intently, with tilted head, at something to the north.

With heart in throat, she followed the direction of the boy's gaze.

The sound she made was like the whimper of a helpless cornered animal. Torn looked north, too, out past the corner of the boxcar-depot, and saw the way-off wisp of dust.

"Looks like a dust devil," he remarked.

"No," she sighed. "The devil's dust."

"Train's comin'!" yelled Case. "I can feel her now!"

"Thank God in heaven," breathed the woman.

"Look," said Torn earnestly. "I don't mean to press the issue, ma'am, but if you're in trouble, I'd be obliged if you'd permit me to help."

"Why?" she asked bluntly.

The corner of Torn's mouth curled, the semblance of a smile.

"Let's just say you remind me of someone I once knew."

"No!" She said it sharply. Then she tried to salve any bruised feelings her curtness might have caused with a smile as gentle as a summer morning rain. Torn's thoughts turned, agonizingly, to another woman, one he had known and loved so many years ago. Another woman who had a sweet and winsome smile.

"No, please," she implored Torn and Schuyler. "You dare not get involved. You're both good men, I'm sure, and brave. But if you help me, you'll answer to Ike Dobson himself. It would be a kindness that could get you killed."

"Ike Dobson!" exclaimed Schuyler, eyes widening. "I knew it. Then, you must be..."

"Ike's wife. Mary Dobson. Chubb is my maiden name. I'm running away from Ike. And he's coming after me. May God have mercy on any man who stands in his path, because *he* won't."

Now Schuyler was casting a longing glance down the line. Immense relief washed across his weathered face as he spotted a ribbon of engine smoke.

"If I were younger, or stronger..." he began, apologetic.

"That's not it." She smiled. "You have a son to look after."

"Yes. He's all I have. His mother passed away some years back. Well, I'd best go drop the highball. They won't stop 'less I do."

Embarrassed by what he judged to be his own cowardice, Schuyler turned quickly away, making for the pole at the edge of the platform, where the large red-metal signal ball was suspended by a chain on block and tackle.

Mary looked at Torn. He was watching the speck of dust far across the tallgrass prairie.

"It's quite all right," she said. "I understand. Believe me, I do. I know very well what kind of man Ike Dobson is, and what he is capable of."

"They're a good hour away, yet," he murmured. "By the time they get here, we'll be on the train and gone. They won't catch a train on tired horses. How many men ride with your husband?"

"As many as he wants. He might have the whole Bar ID crew with him. And any man who works for Ike must be as handy with a gun as he is with a catch rope."

"We'll see."

His stubbornness exasperated her. "I don't *want* your

help. Can't you understand that? There's nothing you can do, Mr. Torn. Except get yourself killed. I don't want that on my conscience."

"It's my choice. You won't be responsible."

"You just don't know Ike. What my husband wants, he gets. And what he gets, he keeps. It's not that he loves me. He just likes having me around. It doesn't matter if I *want* to be with him. And I don't want to be. I can't bear it any longer. I've seen him do terrible things. Not to me, so much as to others."

With a gasp, she cut herself off. It had all started pouring out. All her bitterness, all her problems. She hadn't meant for that to happen. She had no call burdening this man with her troubles.

Torn's features were coldly resolute.

"I won't abide people being held against their will, unless they've broken the law."

"I *have* broken the law. Ike Dobson's law. That's the only law that matters in this part of Kansas."

"Not anymore," said Torn.

CHAPTER 3

TWENTY MINUTES LATER, THE WESTBOUND TRAIN pulled abreast of the Pitchfork Slough depot.

The water tower with its adjacent windmill pump stood just to the west of the station, so that when the locomotive stopped next to it, the first two passenger cars—the Pullman and the day coach—were right alongside the platform. While the train took on water, some of the passengers disembarked, wanting to use the fifteen-minute stop to escape the stale air and hard benches.

Mary Dobson boarded the day coach immediately, with one last anxious look to the north.

Torn carried his saddle to the baggage car. The baggage handler rolled the big freight door open. Torn hefted the saddle up to him, after removing the Winchester from its scabbard.

"Got a couple of stock cars at the tail end," remarked the railroader affably. "Carrying a consignment of cavalry remounts to Fort Dodge. But you may be able to get your horse on one of them."

"My horse," said Torn, "is buzzard bait."

The freightman turned into the car to stash the saddle. Torn took a few steps away, carrying rifle and hand valise, then swung back around to sweep the lengths of the two slat-sided livestock cars with bleak eyes.

The memories rushed headlong at him. They were unpleasantly vivid. The years didn't dim them. The summer sun hammered his broad shoulders, but he felt cold clean through, remembering another train ride taken a long time ago. That had been on the Northern Central, through Maryland's rolling farmland. He had been stuffed into a boxcar, similar to the two he now surveyed, with a hundred other Confederate prisoners taken at the Battle of Gettysburg. It was still all too clear in his mind. The suffocating heat of early August, the gnawing hunger in his belly, the burning agony of the festering gunshot wound in his left thigh. A wound that still, at times, gave him trouble. Worst of all had been the bitter bile of defeat and captivity.

That train ride had been nothing compared to the subsequent torment of the Point Lookout prison camp. But he looked back on the train with particular ill will, for it had been the beginning of sixteen months of pure hell.

He turned sharply away and was making for the day coach when the conductor, quartering across the platform from the boxcar-depot, intercepted him.

"Excuse me, sir. Are you Clayton Torn? *Judge* Clayton Torn?"

"I am."

An ingratiating smile appeared beneath the sweeping black wings of the railroader's mustache. He was a sturdily built man of Irish stock, with a round and ruddy face. In the hierarchy of men who worked the iron road, the post of conductor was the ultimate distinction. He was the captain of the train crew. He wore a blue Prince Albert suit and an A,T & SF pillbox cap on his head.

"I saw your name on the passenger list. Welcome aboard, Your Honor. I noticed that you took a berth in second class. We have a Pullman, Judge Torn. On behalf of the Atchison, Topeka & Santa Fe, I would like to invite you to move forward. At no additional charge, of course."

"I'll manage fine in the day coach."

"Well, if you change your mind . . ."

"I won't."

Torn moved on. He knew why the offer had been made. It was in every railroad's best interest to extend an extra measure of courtesy to those passengers who held positions of authority or influence. It was graft, of a sort. Some would say it was a harmless sort. But Torn would have none of it, and he left the conductor without another word.

Watching Torn walk away, the conductor reviewed in his mind what he knew about the man. A hard-as-nails circuit judge. The bearer of law to remote towns beyond the reach of state and district courts. It was said that Clayton Torn had no patience with the finer points of jurisprudence. That he dispensed with the technical niceties when they failed to suit him. They said Torn's law was Old Testament. An eye for an eye, a tooth for a tooth. A life for a life. Wrongdoers could expect no mercy in his court.

Boarding the day coach by the rear platform, Torn paused just inside the car. He always took it slow and careful when entering a strange place. Now he gave the coach and its occupants a long study.

There was a wood-burning stove at the far end—unstoked, of course, in the dead heat of summer. The two rows of wooden seats were virtually empty; most of the passengers had stepped out to stretch their legs.

A couple of soldier boys had stayed aboard. They sat up front, wearing the blue uniform Torn was still learning to look upon with impassivity. He assumed they were heading back to some dreary frontier post, their furloughs misspent. A woman, plain and sad-faced, looking older than her years, cradled a crying infant. A man who looked like a whiskey drummer—or maybe a Bible salesman—was lying half-prone across one of the benches, sound asleep and sawing logs.

And then there was Mary Dobson, sitting on the last bench to his left as he stepped inside.

"I thought perhaps you'd had second thoughts," she said, "and decided to wait for the next train."

"No, ma'am."

He sat across the aisle from her, on the last bench to the right of the door. When possible, he preferred to sit with no one behind him. He slid the hand valise under the bench.

Passengers began to trickle back in. Torn figured that after one look at Pitchfork Slough, nobody would want to miss the "all-aboard."

The conductor came by. Mary detained him.

"How much longer will we be here?"

The conductor brandished a Waterbury keywinder from his vest pocket and consulted it. "A few more minutes, ma'am. We won't dally. Already half an hour behind schedule, due to an unfortunate accident in Emporia. We were taking on two stock cars. A switchman was crushed between the drawbars."

"That does sound unfortunate," commented Torn, with the merest trace of sarcasm. "One might even say tragic."

"Yes, tragic is a fair description. But not uncommon. I don't mean to sound callous. It's the nature of the job.

Few switchmen retire whole and undamaged. I was one myself for some years, and lucky to walk away intact. Moved up to brakeman. Safer, but only by degree. Riding up top in all kinds of weather. I lost more than one friend on black and stormy nights, when the rain slicked the running boards, or the sleet laid ice an inch thick, and some poor soul lost his footing, and then his life beneath the steel."

"Sounds like you're accustomed to danger."

"Aye. What railroader isn't?"

"Good." Torn glanced out his window, and north across the tallgrass prairie. He didn't see the dust, but then the glass was covered with soot.

"Yes," said the talkative Irishman. "Railroading is a risky business. My first day on the job, I recall the yardmaster telling me to get my supper before starting work. 'There's a better than middling chance you'll get killed,' he told me, 'and I wouldn't want you to make that long trip to hell on an empty stomach.'"

Torn almost smiled. A long trip to hell on an empty stomach. That was an apt description of his experience aboard the Yankee prison train.

The conductor moved forward. A couple of men in rough frontier clothes stalked by, revolvers stuck in their belts. An older couple entered next. The man had the harried look of a shopkeeper or banker. The woman wore the pinched and disapproving expression of a stern, sharp-tongued harridan. Another soldier boy dragged in to join the other two.

"What's taking so long?" breathed Mary, her voice edgy with agitation.

"Don't worry," said Torn, knowing the advice was wasted. She was on the brink of panic. He half-expected her to bolt, and tried to decide on his best course of action if she did so. Every minute seemed like an hour to her now; she was beyond the help of comforting words.

She remained seated a moment more. And then she was up and reaching for the door. She never made it out of the day coach. As she started out, a man came charging in. They collided. With a small cry, Mary lost her balance and fell backwards. She struck the edge of the bench she had just vacated and sat down hard on the floor between the seats.

He stood there a moment, startled, staring dumbly down at her. A lean man in a frayed dove-gray claw hammer coat and white panama hat, he sported a pencil-thin mustache. His eyes were those of a coyote on a chicken house raid. He reeked of French Quinine and pomade. As he recovered from his surprise, his sharp and furtive features turned ugly.

"Next time, why don't you watch where you're going?" he sneered.

Rising swiftly, Torn laid his shoulder squarely into the man's back between the shoulder blades, driving him into the door frame. Stunned, the man staggered backward and tripped over Torn's well-placed leg. He sprawled in the aisle.

"You clumsy son of a bitch!" he snarled.

"You're one to talk."

The man's coyote eyes flicked to Torn's waist. When he saw no evidence of weapons, he got bolder.

"I ought to teach you a lesson."

"You never learned yours."

The man clambered to his feet. Torn pegged him for a cardsharp. Gamblers were as thick as fleas on the railroads these days. The tinhorn turned and bent to retrieve his hat. Torn saw his right arm move, but he couldn't see what that hand was reaching for. It wasn't the hat.

Someone from farther forward yelled a warning.

"Look lively! He's got a gun!"

CHAPTER 4

AS THE MAN SWUNG AROUND TO FACE TORN ONCE more, Torn saw the little over-and-under derringer.

He lashed out, clamping steel-laced fingers on the man's wrist, twisting sharply. With a howl of pain the tinhorn jackknifed forward. Torn maintained a bone-bending grip on the arm, gave it a good hard shake. The hideout clattered to the floor. Bent over double, the gambler saw it through a film of tears. He groped for it with his free hand. Torn drove a knee into his face, hard enough to stun, not hard enough to break anything. Then he slammed the cardsharp into the door frame. The man grunted and sagged. But when he felt the edge of a tempered steel blade caress his Adam's apple he straightened right up, eyes bulging.

"I'm trying hard not to kill you," murmured Torn. "If I catch you being disrespectful to a lady again, I'll stop trying."

"Yes, sir." The man injected each word with a full measure of respect. "I mean, no, sir."

The blade came away from his throat. He caught only a fleeting glimpse of it. Not an ordinary knife. No, more awe inspiring than any garden variety frontier toothpick. The hilt, complete with single-guard bow, resembled that of a cavalry saber. The blade was almost two inches wide, at least fifteen inches long. The tinhorn didn't need to feel its cold touch a second time to testify that it was as sharp as a barber's straight razor.

Keeping his painful grip on the man's wrist, Torn marched him out through the doorway, spun him around, and straight-armed him against the brass railing of the platform.

"Get off the train," said Torn.

"You got no right . . ." began the gambler. The indignation melted away as he got a closer look at Torn, whose tall, wide-shouldered leanness filled the doorway—and at the peculiar edge tool in Torn's hand.

"Get off, or get thrown off."

The gambler watched Torn sweep back the frock coat, and saw the shoulder-rigged leather sheath. He stared as Torn slipped the saber-knife into it. A thong fit over the pommel, and held the weapon snug and upside down, tight against the left side of Torn's ribcage.

"My things are in there. My gun."

"They'll be waiting for you in Wichita."

Since Torn had put the blade away, the cardsharp was pretty well convinced that he wasn't going to be killed on the spot. Humiliation prodded him into boldness.

"This isn't the end of it, mister. The last card hasn't been dealt yet. No one messes with Dice Fontane and . . ."

He ended the threat with a screech of protest as Torn hit him. He didn't even see the punch coming, but he felt it all the way down to the soles of his feet. Torn caught him before he careened over the railing and down onto the coupling. Blood leaked from a split lip.

The conductor was passing alongside the train, his Irish brogue heavy as he sang out the "All aboard!" Torn interrupted his progress by hurling the injured, groggy card-sharp off the platform and right into his path. Fontane landed on his face, and lay there moaning. The Irishman stared up at Torn.

"If he comes back aboard, I'll kill him," said Torn.

"I'll see that he doesn't," promised the conductor.

Torn went back inside the day coach.

Mary Dobson had regained her seat and her composure. The other passengers watched Torn with cautious curiosity as he searched the floor for the hideout. He couldn't find it. Mary's hands were clasped tightly in her lap. They parted, and she held one hand out, palm up. The derringer was in it. Torn now had the leisure to identify the weapon as a double-barreled .22 caliber Frank Wesson with ivory grips.

"I believe this is what you're looking for," she said.

He made no move to confiscate the gun.

"Perhaps you should hold on to it for a while."

"The thought did cross my mind."

"Are you acquainted with firearms, ma'am?"

"I can manage, thank you. But go ahead and take it. It doesn't belong to me. Unlike my husband, I'm not one to take what isn't mine. It belongs to the gentleman you just . . . um . . . removed."

Torn said, "Some say that possession is nine points of the law."

"That's my husband's kind of law," she said dryly.

Every time she spoke of her husband it was with contempt, and fear. Torn was curious, but too polite to ask the very direct questions that sprang to mind.

So he said nothing. Nor did he take the derringer. He returned to the bench across the aisle from her. Mary gave him a sidelong glance. If he noticed, he didn't show it, watching instead the other passengers.

She found it remarkable that this stranger was bound and determined to protect her, regardless of the danger; he was willing to do this knowing only that she was running away from her husband. He looked capable enough. He had handled the gambler without difficulty. But alone he stood absolutely no chance against the fury that was coming hard at them, hell-for-leather across the prairie.

He will surely die, she thought. *And his blood will be on my hands . . .*

CHAPTER 5

THE STATION AGENT, SCHUYLER, APPROACHED THE Baldwin 2–6–0 mogul locomotive as the fireman finished applying liquid tallow from a long-spout can to the engine's steam cylinders. The "tallow pot" swung around off the starboard running board and into the cab, and Schuyler climbed up onto the apron after him. The engineer was taking his ease in the right-side chair, watching his gauges.

"You're running late, Brice," remarked the agent.

The engineer only half-turned his soot-smeared face, but it was enough for Schuyler to see the grim scowl.

"Hello, Schuyler. We had a problem at Emporia."

"Yeah," said the fireman, who was younger and less taciturn than Brice. "Did you know a switchman named McLaughlin?"

"Can't say that I did, personally." Belatedly, the agent realized the significance of the tense. "Wait a minute! What d'you mean, *did* I know?"

"Got himself killed. Crushed between a couple of cars." The fireman paled beneath smudges of ash as he thought back on it.

"That's too bad," muttered the agent over the pipe clenched in his teeth. It was a mild reaction, but heartfelt, all the same; Schuyler had a thick skin.

"I'll say it's too bad," grumbled Brice.

"Maybe you can make up the time," suggested the agent, trying to steer the conversation away from the subject of the dead switchman.

"I'm not one to pound an engine."

Schuyler willed himself not to search the northern horizon for that telltale rise of dust. *Maybe you should, Brice,* he thought. *Just this one time.*

"Thank Christ for that," added the stoker. "It was a happy day when I drew Brice."

Brice snorted, trying not to look pleased. "The poor lad's last engineer kept the stops pulled out."

"Yeah," grinned the boyish fireman. "I was throwing wood so fast you'd have thought my dear old mother was buried alive at the bottom of the tender."

"Well, you're watered up," said Schuyler. "And the line's clear ahead."

"I hope so," muttered Brice. "But I got a bad feeling, Schuyler. Like the thing back at Emporia wasn't the last of it. You know how it is, sometimes. A run can be jinxed from the first 'all aboard.'"

Schuyler's thoughts flew to Mary Dobson. He owed it to these fellow railroaders to alert them to the possibility that there might be trouble. But he hesitated. Why add to Brice's anxiety? If they pulled out now, all would be well.

"Let's go," Brice told the fireman, "while the box is hot."

The fireman laid on the whistle, three sharp tugs.

Schuyler heard the conductor call the last "all aboard," responding to the signal from the Baldwin mogul. Brice let out a bit on the throttle, and the steel behemoth began to breathe faster. The agent felt the pulse of barely leashed power pound up through the floorplate and into his body. He could remember the vivid thrill of riding the iron horse; he had once been an engineer, like Brice, and had spent many good years on the "four-dollar-side" of the cab.

But this was one ride he didn't mind missing, for he couldn't stop thinking that Mary Dobson was a disaster waiting to happen.

"Goin' on to Wichita, Schuyler?" asked Brice.

"Good luck," said Schuyler fervently, and climbed down.

The passengers had boarded. Schuyler joined his son on the platform. Case was fascinated by the agility of the two brakemen, who leaped from car to car atop the train, releasing the hand brakes, one working his way back from the coal tender, the other moving forward from the crow's nest.

Smoke billowed from the diamond-stack. With the release of the Johnson bar, the big red wheels of the mogul began to spin, screeching on rail-steel, then finding purchase. The train inched forward. Schuyler searched the windows of the day coach, compelled to catch one last look at the woman. But he didn't see her. The conductor waved from the Pullman's front platform. A moment later the caboose passed the depot. Rapidly picking up speed, the train charged up the line. They stood, father and son, side by side, and listened to the thunder diminish, until all that remained to fill the vast and heavy silence of the lonesome prairie was the wailing of the wind and the yapping of a dog back among the soddies of Pitchfork Slough.

Schuyler breathed a long sigh of relief.

"I'd best go send the signal, Case," he said, and turned to the boxcar-depot.

He almost collided with Dice Fontane in the doorway, and took a step back, startled as much by the tinhorn's bloodied countenance as by his very presence.

"What in blazes are you doing here?" the agent demanded.

"I was beaten up and thrown off the train," said Fontane, with all the bruised dignity he could muster. "By some tall bastard in black. And none of your colleagues came to my aid—a fact which I'm sure your superiors will be interested to know."

Schuyler gave him a jaundiced look; he was in no mood for threats.

"Man in black, you say? Well, that would be Judge Torn. Were I you, I'd feel damn lucky just to be alive."

"When does the next westbound come through?"

"Be an emigrant train, sometime tonight. A widderwoman runs a bit-house, of sorts, over yonder."

"I'm a tad short of funds at the moment," confessed Fontane.

"Hmm. Slim pickings, huh? You got your 'bible' with you, don't you?"

Fontane took a deck of white-backed pasteboards from a coat pocket, a conniving light aglimmer in his coyote eyes. "Would you be interested in . . ."

Schuyler shook his head emphatically. "I would not. I don't take chances. But the widder-woman might play for drinks. 'Course, if you try to bottom-deal on her, she'll like as not put a hole in you with her old Colt's Dragoon. And if you lose, you might have to 'entertain' her for the afternoon."

Fontane grimaced and Schuyler suppressed a grin.

"Got to telegraph the next station up-line," he said,

brushing past the gambler and going inside.

A few minutes later, done with that chore, Schuyler came back out to find the cardsharp gone.

Case came running up to him.

"Do you hear it, Pa? Sounds like thunder."

Schuyler frowned. Years of riding a locomotive had impaired his hearing. He glanced up at the sky. The furnace sun had bleached most of the blue out of heaven. There wasn't a cloud in sight.

"I think it's shaggies, Pa," said Case. "A bunch of 'em."

"Ain't many buffalo left in these parts," said Schuyler, the hard fist of fear punching at his heart.

He walked to the edge of the platform and looked north. He saw a long drift of dust, quite close now. But the riders were hidden in a fold of the prairie. Now he could hear the thunder of hooves. With the perfect clarity of hindsight, he realized that he should have put himself and his son aboard that westbound, after all. At least then he would have had company in the valley of the shadow.

He heard Case behind him, bare feet slapping the planks of the depot platform, and he said, with taut control, "Case, I want you to go across the track and into the slough."

"What?"

"You heard me. Get on into the slough. Stay down low. And don't you come out until I tell you to. D'you hear, boy? No matter what happens. No matter what you see or hear. Don't you come out till I give the all-clear."

"Pa..." The boy's voice was pitched high and tight.

"Do as I say, Case!"

Case took off running. He paused once, trembling, to look back, standing between the sun-silvered rails.

"Go on," said Schuyler gently.

Case ran.

The thunder filled Schuyler's ears. He felt suddenly old

and weak and alone. He started for the boxcar-depot, but they arrived before he got there. The dust drifted over him, wind-borne, and he tasted grit. The horses pranced and blew, hard-pushed and hard-checked, lathered up from a long run, and with a wild light in their eyes. He heard the jingle of spurs, the creak of saddle leather. They were on both sides of the platform, with a couple more urging their mounts up the siding and onto the track behind him. Schuyler prayed that his son had made the slough, and that Case now lay hidden among the tule that grew there, tall in the soggy ground.

Their hats were pulled down tight and low, and he couldn't see their eyes in the black shadows cast by turned down brims.

6

THE MINUTE THAT PASSED SEEMED LIKE AN ETERNITY to Schuyler. He was almost relieved when one rider spurred his horse forward, to the steps on the east end of the platform. The horse balked, but the rider used his quirt savagely, and kept the animal's head up with a harsh command of rein leather. So ruthlessly driven, the horse had no choice but to take the steps. Steelshod hooves clattered on the planking.

Schuyler willed himself to stand stock still and look steadily back at the mounted man who glowered down at him.

"Where's the woman?"

A gruff voice, both loud and soft at the same time, with the cutting edge of brutal authority. It grated on Schuyler's nerves like the sound of a rusty gate hinge.

The station agent knew there was no profit in trying to mislead this man. The thoroughbred sorrel, still tethered at the rear of the depot, was damning evidence.

"She boarded the westbound to Wichita."

"You know who she is?"

"No."

"You know who I am?"

"No."

The man settled back in his saddle. His body was thick brawn, exuding strength and stamina. His rust-colored hair was dusted with gray. His square, brown face was as hard and craggy as mountain granite.

"You're a goddamned liar," he decided.

"Get down off that horse and say that again," snapped Schuyler, surprising himself.

The man snorted contempt at this bravado.

"I'm Ike Dobson. Now you know who I am?"

"I'm in Kansas, ain't I?"

"This is my land. And that red horse over there is mine, too. What were your plans for that red horse?"

"The lady said someone would be along to fetch it."

"The lady." This time Dobson grunted. "Didn't you heed the brand?"

"Didn't bother. It's none of my business."

"Yes it is. Whether you want it or not."

One of the other riders dismounted. He climbed up onto the platform and strolled forward. His spurs raked the planking. The wind whipped his white duster against long, chap-sheathed legs. He gave Schuyler a big smile. Schuyler knew it was counterfeit—a smile no man in his right mind would trust.

"She *was* after the train, Pa," this one remarked to Ike Dobson. "Just like you said. It ain't gone far. I can still smell it. Let's get a move on. I don't want to miss the fun. I wish I'd gone with Drew when you split us up."

"Our horses are this side of windbroke, Lute," said

Dobson gruffly. "Your brother can stop the train right enough, without our being there."

Schuyler studied Lute Dobson's face: small eyes beneath a straight and uninterrupted line of bushy brow, a broad nose, a thick-lipped mouth that always seemed to be moving, even when he wasn't talking. The agent saw depravity there. It was the face of a man who could be cruel for cruelty's sake. Now it had a petulant cast.

"That ain't fair, Pa."

"Fair?" Dobson leaned forward in the saddle, his body bunched up, his tone scolding. "You think this is a game, boy?"

"No, Pa. I just thought . . ."

"Don't care what you thought. You don't give a tinker's damn about your mother. Never did."

"She ain't my mother. My mother's dead."

"She's your mother now, dammit. But you ain't interested in getting her back. You wouldn't mind if she never set foot on the Bar ID again. All you hanker for is the chance to hurt somebody."

"You ought not to say such in front of the men." Lute's smile chilled into a hard and resentful grimace.

"I'll say what I please, where and when I please."

Lute masked his real feelings and flashed a lazy grin.

"Sure, Pa. Don't let your water boil. It ain't worth it. She's just a squaw, when you get right down to the quick."

Snarling through clenched teeth, Dobson used rein and spur to spin his bay horse half around, and lashed out with his right leg. Lute jumped back, but he wasn't fast enough. Dobson's boot caught him high in the chest and sent him sprawling. Lute's hat came off. The wind plucked it up and carried it off the platform, through the ring of riders.

"I got two sons," hissed Dobson. "I can spare one."

Lute got up and brushed himself off. He was still smiling.

But behind that smile was a hatred as cold and lethal as saber steel.

"Perhaps I can be of assistance," a new voice spoke in the silence.

Schuyler and the Dobsons turned to stare at Dice Fontane as the gambler squeezed through the rank of horsemen and mounted the platform. He had Lute's hat in hand, and returned it to the younger Dobson. Then he looked up at a scowling Ike Dobson with a toad-eating smile.

"Who the hell are you?" barked Dobson.

"Dice Fontane, sir, at your service. I couldn't help but overhear. I saw the woman. Your wife. She got on that westbound train."

"Tell me something I don't know or get out of my air."

"She met a man here. They're traveling together."

Dobson's eyes got as bleak as a blue norther. "What man?"

"His name is Torn. He's a judge, apparently."

"He's a dead man."

"This man is lying!" exclaimed Schuyler, staring angrily at the sly tinhorn. "He has a grudge against Torn. That's why he . . ."

"You know a helluva lot now," growled Dobson, "for somebody who didn't know squat a minute ago."

Schuyler clamped his mouth shut.

Dobson scanned the circle of grim-set riders. "Charley Leech!"

"Yessir, Mr. Dobson."

"Shoot that bluegrass stallion."

"Yessir, Mr. Dobson."

The rider pulled out of line, drawing his saddle-gun from its boot. He rode around behind the boxcar-depot. A half-minute later the rifle spoke, a single sharp report that was quickly shredded and carried off by the wind.

"That's what happens," Dobson icily informed Schuyler, "to anything and anyone who helps my wife run away. Now, you and I, we're gonna go inside, and you're gonna send a message on your talking wire to the Bellefoot station. Y'see, my oldest, Drew, is waitin' to hear from me. We're gonna tell him to stop that train and get my wife. And we'll also tell him to kill this bastard Torn."

"What makes you think I'll help you?" asked Schuyler.

The rider returned to line, the stock of his saddle-gun braced against his thigh.

"He's down, Mr. Dobson."

Dobson's eyes were boring into Schuyler.

"Don't boot that rifle yet, Charley," he said. "You've still got work to do."

CHAPTER 7

LISTENING TO THE CLACK AND CLATTER OF THE train on the rails, Torn was staring out the window when a thought struck him. He cast speculative eyes at the telegraph line that ran parallel to the tracks, two strands of wire looping from post to post. He glanced at Mary Dobson. She had been watching him, and looked quickly away, only to realize that she had been caught, and smiled sheepishly.

"I didn't mean to stare."

"Your husband," he said. "Smart man?"

"Cunning. He leaves nothing to chance."

Torn nodded, reached under his bench and slid the heavily-packed hand valise forward between his legs. Unstrapping it, he removed a gunbelt and extracted a short-barreled pistol from a well-oiled holster. Thumbing the hammer back, he rolled the cylinder down his sleeve, checking the loads. Then he eased the hammer down, slipped the gun back into the holster.

"What is that?" she asked.

"Peacemaker, .45 caliber. Colt started manufacturing it a couple of years ago. The most reliable pistol on the market."

"I know *what* it is. I've been around guns all my life. I guess what I meant to ask was why did you take it out?"

"That little .22 might get you out of a scrape with a hostile jackrabbit, ma'am, but I wouldn't rely on it for much more."

"If you're going to risk your life on my account, you could at least stop calling me 'ma'am.'"

"Mrs. Dobson?"

"I don't care if I ever hear that name again. Too many bad memories. Oh, I do wish I could wake up one day and just forget all that's happened. No, call me Mary, please."

"Mary, then."

"You said I reminded you of someone you once knew."

He looked away. "We all have bad memories."

He lay the holstered Colt on the bench beside him, heeled the valise back under and out of the way and, saying no more, resumed his study of the passing countryside.

Mary stifled her curiosity. Clearly, he wished to leave that subject alone.

Half an hour later, Torn chanced a look across the aisle. Mary had slipped down on the bench, resting her head against the frame of the window beside her. Her hazel eyes were closed. He took the opportunity to gaze at her unabashedly. She was a beauty. A faint and melancholy smile touched a corner of his mouth.

He slipped a hand under his black frock coat, took the daguerreotype out of his inside breast pocket. That all-too-familiar emptiness swept over him as he gazed at the full-length studio photograph of Melony Hancock. How many times a day did he gaze at her image? How many days in all the years since he had last seen her in the flesh? This was all he had left of her. This, and a few old letters. Some of the silver coating on the daguerreotype's copper plate had worn away. He carried it always in the breast pocket, over his heart. Admittedly, it was a trite sentimental gesture. But he refused to let go of the hope that someday he would find the woman he loved.

The war had taken her from him. They had been engaged—Charleston's most beautiful and desirable belle and a blue-blood son of the South—during that glorious summer of '61, when the Confederacy stood newborn before the world in all its naive glory. That same summer he had marched north to fight the good fight, an officer in a regiment of South Carolina's volunteer cavalry. Like all the other boys in gray, he had been confident of quick victory. They had grievously underestimated the determination of a backwoods president—and the Yankees in general—to preserve the Union.

Looking back on it, Torn wondered at his foolishness. Going off to fight, and possibly to die, for principles that now seemed remote and indefinable, when he'd had everything to live for. His father was a wealthy planter, as had been his father before him, and Torn stood as an established member of the landed gentry, not to mention a brilliant student of the law at the prestigious University of Virginia. And last, but by no means least, he had been the future husband of Melony Hancock.

All that was lost in the rubble of a lost cause collapsing. His family killed, the vast Torn holdings destroyed by torch and theft during Sherman's March to the Sea and the subsequent Occupation, in many ways more devastating than the war itself. Everything was in ruins; worst of all, his fiancée was now missing in the confusion. Scanty evidence indicated that Yankee deserters had abducted her.

Torn liked to think that he was a realist. Any man who came out of a Northern prisoner-of-war camp alive after sixteen months of captivity, as he had, was certainly nothing if not a realist. But a realist would accept the likelihood that Melony was dead. After years of following false leads, a realist would bury the past and give up the search.

But here he was, pursuing another lead. It was this relentless search for Melony that was taking him to Wichita. He had a smattering of friends; one operated the Lady Gay, a Wichita thirst emporium. Ted Judah's letter had chased him down in a jerkwater town up along the Vermilion. Torn had immediately set out. After losing his horse, he'd legged it to Pitchfork Slough to catch the first available westbound.

He didn't have high hopes of finding Melony in Wichita, despite Judah's information that a woman who looked like the angel in the daguerreotype had appeared there. Torn recalled remarking to Schuyler that his business in Wichita wasn't urgent. Now, *that* was a realist talking. Maybe he was chasing a ghost. Or his own past. Just maybe, in a dark corner of his mind, he equated finding Melony with recapturing a happier time.

One thing was certain. The *original* Clayton Randall Torn, gentleman and officer, who had ridden up those oak-lined, red-dirt, tidewater roads to Virginia battlefields, full of the adventure of the moment with the bright prospects of the future shining in his young eyes—*that* man had been a casualty of the late War Between the States. There was nothing left of that man but a hard and empty shell.

And so he kept searching...

When the flurry of gunshots rang out, Mary Dobson nearly jumped out of her skin.

From the moment she had slipped out of the Bar ID ranch house, saddled her favorite Kentucky horse, and ridden away with only the clothes on her back, she had known, deep down inside, that there was really no escape from Ike Dobson. From the very beginning she had expected the worst, and had tried to prepare herself. Still, with the end now at hand, she panicked.

"Oh, God!" It was a soft, strangled sob, lost in the shouting tumult of the other passengers in the day coach.

She came out of her seat like a cinch-bound bronc feeling saddle weight for the first time. Even though there was nowhere to run, she had to try. She spun toward the rear door—and right into Torn's arms. She looked up into calm, gray eyes.

"I'd advise against going out just now," he said.

"I've got to!" she cried, pulling back, her control cracking under the strain. "Don't you understand? I've got to! Innocent people could get hurt. Even killed. I've seen enough of that. I can't bear to see any more. I don't want any more on my conscience."

Torn didn't try to hold her, but neither did he cease to block the door.

"Don't give up, Mary."

He saw a solitary tear slip down her cheek, and felt sorry for her. He wanted to comfort her, but made no move to touch her again. There was still a vestige of the Southern gentleman in him, despite all the hard years spent in rough company.

"No," she said, gathering emotional strength from Torn's stony calm. "No, I won't give up. He can drag me back. He can beat me. But he'll have to kill me to keep me from running away again, and then again after that."

Her words sparked cold flame in Torn's eyes. Those had been his sentiments many years ago, when a sadistic Yankee prison guard had tried to break his stubborn pride. But pride had been all that was left to Torn in that hell on earth called Point Lookout, and he would have died rather than relinquish it. He was proud of Mary, and felt drawn to her, now that she had said those words.

There was another ragged burst of gunfire. Mary sank back onto the bench.

"What do we do?" she asked, the derringer gripped in one white-knuckled fist.

"Stay low. Let them play their hand. Then we'll play ours."

CHAPTER 8

THE FIRST VOLLEY HAD BEEN FIRED SKYWARD, FROM the pistols and saddle-guns of ten riders who kept their horses in a tight cluster ranged across the tracks. They had swarmed out of a hollow and into view, quick as thought.

"Jesus, Brice!" howled the young fireman. In the process of throwing wood into the firebox, he hurled himself into the left-side chair, so that he could get a clear view past the long snout of the locomotive at the track ahead.

"Dammitalltohell!" exploded Brice. "I knew there'd be more grief. I just knew it."

"It's a hold-up!" bleated the fireman.

"Your first, I take it."

"Will you pound it, Brice? Just this once?"

"That's my intent. Now get off your duff and keep stoking."

The fireman began throwing wood with more enthusiasm than Brice had ever seen displayed by a single individual.

He eased the throttle bar full open and pulled the whistle chain.

The horses were nervous enough with the Baldwin mogul bearing down on them. When the earsplitting scream of the steam whistle slashed the air they began to give the men who rode them serious argument.

Brice smiled. It looked like a bronc-busting free-for-all.

"I guess they figured we'd stop was they to hold a cutthroat convention in the middle of our railroad," he commented.

"God's sake, don't stop!" gasped the stoker as he worked.

"I'll stop in Wichita and not before. If there's a just God in heaven, we'll have one or two of those bravos smeared all over the cowcatcher when we get there."

But the riders separated into two groups on either side of the tracks, gut-hooking their unruly mounts and taking off at a lusty gallop up-road. For one ludicrous moment it looked to Brice like *he* was chasing *them*.

One of the horsemen, bent low in the saddle, twisted around and fired a shot behind him. Brice heard the slug strike the boilerplate. Some of the other riders began to throw lead back at the Baldwin. A bullet smashed the window on the fireman's side. The slug ricocheted through the cab. The stoker fell facedown on the floor.

"Damn!" yelled Brice. "You hit?"

"I ain't," came the muffled reply. The fireman didn't raise his head. "And I don't aim to be."

"Keep stoking," growled Brice.

The fireman reluctantly got up and returned to his labors, jerking every time a slug hit the mogul.

Brice grimaced. "They're gonna try to board," he muttered.

"What?" The pounding roar of the iron and steel behemoth filled the fireman's ears, drowning out the engineer's sober prediction.

Brice didn't bother repeating it.

As the mogul gained on the horsemen, the horses themselves tried to veer away from the rails. The riders used steel bit and spurs to keep them straight on. The cab pulled even with the rearmost rider on the engineer's side. Brice glanced over in time to see the horseman taking aim with his sidegun. He ducked. The bullet shattered window glass. A shard slashed the engineer's cheek. Brice touched his cheek, looked at his fingers, and saw red.

"Sonuvabitch," he muttered.

He reached under his seat with his free hand—the other was gripping the throttle bar. Out came a .44 Dance revolver. Brice stuck the long barrel out through the smashed window and fired. He didn't expect to hit anything but Kansas, the Baldwin shuddering like it was. But shooting back made him feel better.

The rider sawed on the reins, slowing the horse, and dropped back alongside the tender. Looking left, Brice saw another rider on the other side doing the same thing.

"Look out from behind!" he roared.

"What?"

"Hell!" spat Brice, thoroughly disgusted with the way things were developing. "Do I have to stop the damn train just to make myself heard to you? They'll be coming over the tender!"

The stoker finally comprehended. He looked back in time to see a man clambering over the top of the tender. The man's duster was flung straight back away from his body by the whipstream. The fireman raised a length of wood like a club. The man jumped, catching the edge of the cab's roof and swinging his legs forward, punching the fireman in the chest with both booted feet. The stoker was hurled back against the boiler. He struck his head and slumped.

The man landed clumsily, stumbling over the fireman's body. Brice fired a wild shot and let go of the throttle bar. In the close confines of the cab it was hard to miss. The man spun, sprawling across the fireman's seat. Brice whirled as another man descended from the tender to the apron. The engineer saw the gun jump in the man's hand. It was the last thing he ever saw. The bullet punched him in the chest. He slammed back against the boiler, then pitched forward, dead, across the body of the young fireman.

The killer clambered over the bodies. He stood a moment, with mounting frustration, glowering at the profusion of wheel valves, levers, pipe, and gauges adorning the boiler's back end. He looked at the wounded man.

"Did he kill you?"

"Naw, Drew. Just creased me." The other man was clutching his left arm. Blood was leaking through his fingers.

"Then get your butt over here and stop this thing. That's why we brought you along, y'know. It weren't for your charm and good looks."

"Jesus, Drew. You shot the engineer."

"He had a gun. What was I supposed to do?"

"But the railroad..."

"Pa owns the men who own the railroad," snapped Drew, exasperated. "Now are you gonna stop this iron horse or not? What's that godawful smell?"

"The boy's hair's on fire!"

Drew Dobson looked down at the stoker with more

curiosity than concern. Sure enough, the fireman lay so close to the open firebox that the hair on his head was singed, the scalp blistering.

"I'll take care of these two. You stop the train."

"The brakemen must be back in the chummy. It'll take longer without somebody working the hand brakes, Drew."

"Shut up and stop the goddamn train!"

Chastened, the other man took the engineer's chair. He eased back the throttle, shut down the water injectors as quickly as he dared, opened the steam release and worked the Johnson bar.

As the mogul began to slow, Drew dragged the bodies to the apron and pitched them out of the cab.

The other riders swung back alongside the Baldwin. Their cantering horses were agitated by the shooting jets of steam and the hideous screech of steel on steel. Drew gestured sharply.

"Get aboard! What are you waiting for? A damn invitation? You know what we come here to do. Find her. And kill the man who's with her!"

CHAPTER 9

AS THE BALDWIN MOGUL SLOWED, THE CARS BEGAN to jam together like a pressed squeezebox, jolting the passengers.

Torn stood, bracing himself between the wooden benches as he strapped on his gunbelt and looked forward. Pandemonium reigned in the day coach. The infant in the lone woman's arms was squalling. An island of calm in the storm, she was trying to mollify the baby with soft words. Men were shouting, peering out windows, crouching between the seats. One of the characters in the rough frontier attire was striding down the aisle, a fierce scowl on his bearded, sun-darkened face, and an old Remington .44 percussion pistol in his fist. He was muttering obscenities, clamping down on them only when he passed the woman with the child.

Torn stepped out into the aisle. The man stopped and glowered at him.

"Get outa my way," he growled at Torn. "I'll teach these bandits a thing or two."

"They're not hold-up men," said Torn. "They ride for Ike Dobson."

The name knocked the stuffing out of the rough-cut hombre. All the fight went right out of him.

"Ike Dobson, you say? You're not scalping my goat, are you, mister?"

"I'm dead serious. They're after the lady." Torn glanced at her, then added, "And me."

The man looked at them both with consummate pity. "That's tough luck."

Torn said, "If you ache for a fight, we could use the help. But if you're more interested in your health, I suggest you go back and sit down. Belt that thumb-buster and don't make trouble. Tell the others to do the same."

"I wish I could help you folks, but . . . Ike Dobson?" He shook his head emphatically. "I don't mind a good fight, but I ain't one to punch my own ticket."

He turned his back on them and headed for the front of the day coach. Torn grabbed his Winchester, then held a hand out to Mary Dobson. She was pale, but with the thorough calm of one resigned to her fate.

"Time to go," said Torn. "They've got the engine, and they're stopping the train."

"But, how . . . ? You said he couldn't catch us on tired horses."

"This isn't the bunch that raised the dust we saw. Your husband must have split his men into two groups. One followed you to Pitchfork Slough. The other made for the next station up the line, in case you had time to get on this train. My guess is that the first bunch telegraphed ahead."

Mary nodded. "It's just like him. He's not even afraid of the railroad."

"Mary," he said earnestly, "we should go now."

She put her hand in his, and rose. She was still holding onto that hideout.

"What are we going to do?" she asked.

"There are two cars full of horses, cavalry remounts, at the end of the train. We're going to try to get to them."

The car lurched again. The train was slowly grinding to a halt. Torn saw a rider thundering past outside. A woman screamed from the Pullman, the next car forward.

"Let's go," he said. "Stay close behind me."

He went out through the door and paused on the rear platform as another rider galloped past, heading for the rear of the train. A bullet whined past his ear and smacked into the siding of the baggage car that trailed the day coach. It wasn't the rider—he had already disappeared from sight and hadn't noticed them. Torn spun, drawing the Colt Peacemaker, and saw two dusty, gun-toting strangers at the front end of the day coach. One was lining up another shot. The second struck the first's gun arm downward.

"You churnhead fool! You'll hit the woman!"

Out of the corner of one eye, Torn saw Mary's arm come up, locked straight, and before he could state an objection, she had fired the derringer. A man shouted, the matron screamed, and everyone dove for cover, including the two Dobson men coming down the aisle. Mary gave Torn a chilly half-smile.

"That should cool their heels," she said.

"Here," he said, handing her the Winchester. Holstering the Colt, he vaulted both railings and the coupling space between, landing on the front platform of the baggage car.

"The rifle." She threw it to him. He caught it, and with a hard, fast flick of the wrist, worked the lever action one-handed, swept stock to shoulder and sighted back through the open rear door of the day coach.

"Would you mind standing to one side?" he asked her.

She stepped out of his line of fire. The Winchester spoke. The bullet struck the stovepipe of the old iron potbelly at the far end of the car. Raised heads quickly dipped down again.

He held a hand out to her. Mary looked down at the drawbars and the blur of track beneath, steeled herself, and hiked one leg to get a footing on the railing, taking his hand. She jumped, and Torn caught her as she lost her balance. For a brief moment their bodies were pressed together. Then Torn backed away with a mumbled "Beg pardon" and tried the door of the baggage car. It was locked. He wasted no time with knocking, drawing the revolver and firing one shot into the lock, then kicking the door in.

"Christ! Don't shoot! Don't kill me!" The baggage handler wasn't even looking at them. All he knew was that there had been some shooting, and that someone was breaking into the car; all he cared about was escape. He was rolling the big freight door open.

"No!" yelled Torn. "Don't . . ."

But it was too late. The baggage handler dived out through the doorway.

"Look before you leap," muttered Torn. He took Mary's hand again and started for the rear of the baggage car.

The car was fairly empty. There were stacks of eastern newspapers, bundles of new farm implements, neatly stacked piles of forty-pound seed bags, a few trunks and valises—and Torn's saddle. Torn figured he'd retrieve that saddle if and when he made it to Wichita.

They were abreast of the open freight door when the rider Torn had seen a moment before reappeared. He was galloping with the train now, and he looked into the baggage car and saw them. Reining the horse in close, he reached up to grab the long iron of the door's outer handle, kicked out of the stirrups, and let the horse run out from under. He swung his legs up into the car, hooking his spurs into the floor planking. It was a handsome job of boarding thought Torn, as he stepped over and kicked the man in the chest. The impact swung the man back out of the car, but he didn't let go of the handle. His body thumped against the outside of the door. Torn heaved the cumbersome door shut, but before he could get it all the way closed, the man swung his body back around. His right arm hooked around the edge of the door. Torn caught only a brief glimpse of the sidegun before it went off, so close that the flash temporarily blinded him. Grains of burning gunpowder stung his cheek. The bullet missed Torn's head by a tick's hair. His ears ringing from the percussion of the gunshot, Torn slammed the door shut, as hard as he could. The man yelled hoarsely as his arm was crushed. The gun clattered to the floor of the car. Torn pulled the door open a bit and saw the man hit the ground and go somersaulting. Closing the door, he dropped the heavy iron tongue of the latch into place. He picked up the cowboy's gun and tucked it under his belt before rejoining Mary. They exited the baggage car through the rear door.

He saw the fist coming at him and tried to dodge. Knuckles dusted his chin. The Winchester was in his left hand; he brought the barrel up hard into the Bar ID man's midsection. The cowboy doubled over, grunting, but he was range-tough, and quick to recover. Torn threw a punch, but the man was in too close for it to count much. They grappled in the tight confines of the platform. Torn dropped the Winchester; it was of no earthly use to him in this instance. Locked together, they collided with Mary, who fell back into the baggage car. The cowboy gave Torn's kidneys a couple of good punches. Gritting teeth against the excruciating pain of the blows, Torn worked his arm up under the man's chin and pushed against his windpipe, hoping to pry the cowboy off of him.

The whole train convulsed as brakes were applied anew. Torn and the Bar ID man were pitched into the wall of the baggage car. The baggage car slammed forward against its coupling with the day coach, and shunted violently backwards. The recoil threw Torn and the cowboy right over the railing.

Torn heard Mary cry out as he went over. The train was slowing rapidly now, but it was still rolling with sufficient speed to convince him that falling onto the rails was an unhealthy prospect. So he let go of the cowboy and lashed out to grab hold of something. Anything. This turned out to be one of the vertical bars of the railing. The cowboy hit the coupling and slipped off. Hurt badly, he held onto Torn for dear life. Torn knew he couldn't pull them both up and over the railing. He also knew that the railing wasn't going to hold for long with the weight of two men pulling on it. So he struck downward with his free arm, a backhanded blow to the man's face. The cowboy lost his grip and fell, disappearing beneath the first livestock car. Torn tried to close his ears to the terrible scream, abruptly curtailed.

Swinging his long legs up, Torn clambered over the railing. The man's scream had shaken Mary. She was staring at Torn with an anguished expression on her face. He knew what she was thinking: was escape from Ike Dobson worth all these men dying?

"Want to quit?" he asked harshly.

She drew a long, ragged breath. "No. But ... what do we do now?"

He turned to look at the stock car. It had no platform, no means of entry except for freight doors on either side. And they couldn't reach the freight doors.

The two men they had seen in the day coach appeared at the front end of the baggage car. Advancing side by side, they raised their guns and closed in on Torn and Mary Dobson.

CHAPTER 10

TORN KNEW THEIR ONLY CHANCE LAY WITH THE horses in the stock car. They wouldn't get far if they jumped the train and tried to flee on foot. He thought he knew of a way to reach the remounts. Problem was, it would take a little time. And even a little time was more than those two Bar ID cowboys aimed to give them.

He pushed Mary back against the outer wall of the baggage car, motioning for her to stay put. Then he stepped through the doorway, back into the car. The two men pulled up. They both had their sideguns aimed at him.

"Your name Torn?" asked one.

"It is."

"We got orders to kill you."

"Turn around," advised Torn, "and go back where you came from."

"Can't. What Mr. Dobson says to do, we damn well do."

Torn threw himself to the floor, drawing the Peace-maker. He fanned three shots before he hit the floor, and fired the last three on the roll. The cowboys got off one shot apiece. A bullet carved a groove in the floor scant inches from Torn. The other tunneled through the roof, fired as one of the Bar ID men was flung backwards, three .45 slugs punching into his chest. The other cowboy dropped to his knees, hugging himself, shot twice in the gut. As Torn got up, this one pitched forward, vomiting blood.

Stepping back out onto the rear platform, Torn reloaded the Colt. He flicked bleak gray eyes at Mary.

"Your husband is going to answer to me," he said.

"I'm sorry . . ."

Holstering the revolver, he scooped up the Winchester, handed it to her.

"I'm going up onto the roof of the next car. Then you'll toss me the rifle. After that, I want you to sit tight. I'll bring the horse to you."

She nodded. "Be careful."

"This is hardly the time or place for careful."

The train was grinding to a stop. Time was running out. Torn went to the end of the platform and jumped for the grab iron at the corner of the stock car. He got a foot in the metal stirrup and began to climb. Once on the roof, he made a come-ahead gesture, and Mary tossed him the repeater.

As he had hoped, there was a roof hatch at either end of the slat-sided stock car. He tried the closest one, and was not surprised to find it latched from within. Standing, he slammed the stock of the Winchester downward, sev-eral times. The brass buttplate shattered the hatch into jagged splinters of old and weathered wood.

Torn knelt, groped inside, found and undid the latch.

He was lifting what was left of the hatch when a man shouted from somewhere up ahead. A bullet punched through the wood of the hatch and plucked at his sleeve. He glimpsed a man running toward him on top of the Pullman. The man leaped the gap to the day coach, paused, and fired again. But Torn was already dropping through the hatchway. He didn't waste time with the narrow iron ladder, landing in a crouch on the straw-covered floor of the car.

There were twenty remounts in the car, tied to iron pipe riveted to the wall. The horses stood haunch to haunch, ten at this end of the car, ten at the other.

Torn spotted a couple of coiled lengths of Manila hemp on long nails. Taking one of these catch ropes, he went to the nearest animal, a sorrel with three white stockings. He fashioned a loose lark's-head knot dead center of the rope, slipped it over the sorrel's bottom lip, then tied the ends together over the back of the horse. The rope would serve as bridle and rein, Plains Indian-style. He did the same thing with the other rope and the next horse, a sturdy black mare. There was no time to pick and choose; Torn just had to hope that the Army contracted reliable horse buyers who knew a spavined nag when they saw one.

Drawing the saber-knife, he went down the line, cutting the neck ropes of the other remounts.

On the rear platform of the baggage car, Mary stood still as a cigar store Indian, scarcely daring to breathe. She heard men shouting, the drumming of hooves. With a final lurch, the train came to a complete stop. She wondered what was taking Torn so long. Now, more than ever, she wanted to get away, and fast. Not so much for herself as for Torn. He had been forced to kill at least two of Ike's men. Ike demanded absolute loyalty from his cowboys, and gave absolute loyalty in exchange. He would ride to hell and back again to get anyone who killed a Bar ID man.

"Mrs. Dobson."

She gasped, spun her head around, saw the cowboy standing on the siding to her right. He was holding a pistol. It wasn't aimed right at her, exactly, but it was there at the ready.

"Where's the feller who was with you?"

Mary recognized him. An older cowboy named Ned. Smart and tough and a fair hand with a hogleg.

"He . . . he jumped off the train."

Ned pushed his lips out and in, out and in, sun-faded eyes narrowed and wary. Finally, giving a short nod, he holstered the pistol and stepped forward to mount the platform.

"We been sent to bring you home, Mrs. Dobson. Ike misses you something fierce, I reckon."

Mary brought her arm up and across her body. For the first time, Ned saw the hideout, now that it was pointed straight at him. He froze.

"Stay away from me. I'm warning you. Back off."

Ned climbed down and took several backward steps, arms lifted slowly from his sides. Mary heard the thud of booted feet on the roof of the baggage car, and then a familiar voice from overhead.

"What is it, Ned?"

"It's Mrs. Dobson, Drew," replied Ned calmly, watching the derringer. "She's got the drop on me."

"The hell you say!"

Drew jumped from the baggage car to the stock car, from which point he could look down and see Mary.

"Now, mamma," he sneered. "You wouldn't shoot ol' Ned, would you?"

"Don't call me that!" she snapped, vehement.

Drew's sneering smile turned ugly. "Throw down that hideout."

Two men were riding back along the train, on the opposite side from where Ned stood. Seeing Drew on the roof of the first stock car, they checked their horses.

"There she is," Drew called to them, pointing at Mary. "Get her. She can't nail us all with that pocket gun."

The two riders were in the process of dismounting when the freight door on their side rolled open. A couple of gunshots rang out from within. Drew cursed as a bullet tore through the roof, uncomfortably close. He lost his balance and fell, rolling off the roof before he could catch himself, falling to the ground on Ned's side. Mary was distracted for a split second. That was all Ned needed to make a diving leap out from under the derringer.

The remounts came pouring out of the stock car. The two Bar ID riders were directly in the path of this torrent of horseflesh. A cloud of pale yellow dust rose from this melee of snorting animals and yelling men. Mary watched one man go down with his horse. The other had his hands full as his mount commenced to crow-hopping. Horses were galloping off in every direction.

Out of the dust and confusion appeared Torn, riding bareback on the black mare, Winchester in hand, and leading a sorrel up alongside the baggage car platform.

"Ready for a little ride in the country?" he asked her.

CHAPTER 11

TORN AND MARY LET THE HORSES RUN FULL OUT.
They stayed low, but no shots were fired after them. This
surprised Torn; he threw a few over-the-shoulder looks
at the train, and saw no sign of pursuit. Mary kept the
sorrel to his right and a half-length behind, letting him set
the course. She was a natural, born to ride—this he could
tell at a glance.

At first Torn did not concern himself with direction,
giving the black mare her head. He held the Winchester
and the makeshift reins of Manila hemp in his right hand,
and used the neck rope that had once tethered the horse
to the stock car's pipe as a quirt with his left. The mare
stretched out, galloping belly-down, nostrils flaring. The
tall prairie grass brushed Torn's legs.

They rode a mile, and then another. The mare's breathing grew increasingly labored. Torn knew it was a killing
pace, one that even the strongest mustang could not main-

tain much longer, carrying a rider's weight. He pushed on for one more mile before gradually slowing the black to an easy canter. Another mile and he checked the horse and dismounted. Mary followed suit.

"We'll walk them a minute," said Torn.

They walked through the hip-high grass side by side, letting the horses cool down, and scattering grasshoppers with every stride. It was late in the afternoon, and the sun was only the span of a hand above the western horizon on their right, but it was still mercilessly hot, and the dry searing wind served only to make it hotter still.

The prairie stretched out in all directions, a gently rolling sea of grass. At the crest of a fold in the earth, Torn stopped. He and Mary both ran their hands down the legs of their horses, searching for trembles, and found none.

"The cavalry is well-mounted these days," he remarked, satisfied with the quality of the horses.

Mary looked back in the direction of the train. It was still visible, way off in the distance. She shaded her eyes against the lancing, sidelong glare of the lowering sun, trying to spot any pursuit. Torn watched with her. They stood still, their attention riveted to their backtrail, for a full five minutes. The prairie, with the rise and dip of its contour, could be treacherous. A long look was wiser than a hasty glance; a small army could remain unseen for minutes at a time in one of the many hollows between the distant tracks and their vantage point.

Finally, incredulous, Mary said, "I can't believe it. They're not coming after us."

Torn heard a surging rise of renewed hope in her tired voice.

"I don't know Ike Dobson personally," he said, "but I suspect he isn't the kind to give up easy."

"No, you're right. He isn't." She nodded, cautioning herself against the folly of optimism.

Torn turned, carefully scanning the prairie east, south, and west, and doing some quick mental calculations. It was at best a rough estimate, but he figured Wichita lay a good fifty miles toward the setting sun. There were a couple of settlements to the north, but going north meant riding into the heart of Dobson country. As far as he knew, there was nothing south except a two-day ride to the border of the Indian Nations.

It was a safe bet there *would* be pursuit, and more likely sooner than later. A trail through the tallgrass was easier to follow when it was fresh. Torn didn't count nightfall as an ally, either. The night would be clear, with an early three-quarters moon. At best, night would only slow Dobson and his men. It probably wouldn't stop them.

He had to assume they would come hard and fast, as relentless as bloodhounds on a strong spoor. Their only chance was to move fast, too. But to keep up the pace and stay ahead, they and their horses would need water, and soon. The Arkansas River lay somewhere to the southwest. Several tributaries flowed south across the prairie.

"We'll ride west," he decided aloud. "We'll come to water soon if we do. And, if it comes down to a fight before nightfall, we'll have the sun at our backs when we're forced to turn and make a stand."

She stared at him, her gaze intense.

"My home is south. Three days' ride. Neither of us will be safe until I am among my people," she said.

"By home you mean the Nations."

Again she nodded.

"Cherokee?"

"Seminole. I was born in the village of Mikasuki, on the banks of the Canadian."

"And you're betting that Ike Dobson won't follow you into the Nations."

"The Seminole Nation is one place where he is not the law."

"But you caught a train heading west for Wichita."

"I didn't think he would dare stop a train. And I thought I might find someone in Wichita who would help me get home. But now I have you to help me. And a fresh horse. And only three days' ride from my people."

She looked away as she spoke, and Torn sensed that she wasn't telling him everything.

"Your first plan was a good one," said Torn. "I don't think we can stay ahead of them for three days. But we might be able to for one. Long enough to get to Wichita. They'll have fresh mounts, too, if they're smart. There's another carload of cavalry horses on that train."

She turned away. Grabbing a handful of the sorrel's mane, she mounted Indian-fashion.

"All right," she said crisply, submitting reluctantly to his judgment.

He was struck by her beauty. Her hat dangled by its chinstrap down her back. The hard riding had shaken her raven hair loose, so that it fell in thick disarray about her shoulders. Her cheeks were flushed, her eyes bright, and there was a sheen of perspiration on the graceful curve of her upper lip, and in the smooth hollow of her throat.

"Well, are you coming?" she asked.

"I reckon I will," he said wryly, "since I've come this far."

She spun the sorrel around, quirted with the neck rope and took off at a good, ground-eating canter, heading straight into the sun. Torn mounted up and followed. Watching her, in spite of being up to his tonsils in trouble, he felt lucky. Like a man condemned to hang, whose rope breaks on the drop.

CHAPTER

12

WHEN IKE DOBSON REACHED THE TRAIN, TRAILED
by his son Lute and eleven Bar ID riders, the setting sun
had painted the western sky with broad strokes of carmine
red and yellow ocher. The green and tan hues of the prairie
had deepened into blue-streaked amber. But even on the
best of days, Ike Dobson was not the sort to waste time
admiring the handsome glory of the land that stretched
limitless and majestic in every direction.

While those who followed him wore the drawn and haggard look of men pushed to the limit of physical endurance,
Ike, on the other hand, carried himself like a man who
could never be afflicted by mortal concerns like hunger or
thirst, pain or exhaustion.

There were several horses tethered to the metal stirrups and grab irons of the day coach. As Dobson drew
nearer he could see that the saddle cinches had been loos-

ened. Several other horses were scattered across the prairie, some saddled, some not.

Dismounting on the run, Ike reached the rear platform of the day coach, and was confronted by the Bar ID man, Ned.

"Where is she?" snapped Dobson, his voice harsh with trail dust.

"She got away, Mr. Dobson."

Dobson's craggy features contorted as he fought to control a violent rage. Ned was well acquainted with the dangerous temper of his boss, but faced Dobson without flinching.

"Then what the hell are you doing here?" rasped Dobson.

"Come on inside and I'll show you."

Dobson mounted the platform and paused to face the cluster of riders. They were slack in their saddles, on horses that had been pushed so hard and for so long they had the trembles.

"Lute, come with me. The rest of you, light down and walk those horses."

He followed Ned into the day coach, with Lute at his heels.

Three bodies wrapped in blankets were laid out across wooden benches, chap-sheathed legs and booted feet extending out into the narrow aisle.

Dobson noticed that one bundle was blood-soaked, with only one leg extending from it. He stepped closer, saw the massive pool of blood on the floor of the car.

"What happened here?"

"That's Cal, Mr. Dobson," said Ned, stoic. "What's left of him. He fell under the train. Cut one of his legs clean off. He bled to death."

"And these two?"

"Johnny Capps and Shad Morris. Shot."

"Where's Drew?"

"Up front."

Dobson grimly proceeded up the aisle. Near the front of the coach he found one man hunched over on a bench, head down, his arm cradled in a bandanna sling. On the floor near the cold potbelly stove lay another Bar ID cowboy, his chest tightly dressed with what had been a linsey-woolsey shirt. This man was half-conscious, his breathing ragged, his complexion ashen.

"Santee got himself horse-stomped," explained Ned. "He's all broke up inside, and halfway across the river."

"I can see that," said Dobson curtly.

He turned to see Drew sprawled on a bench. His son looked like he was sleeping. His breathing was deep and regular. There was no outward evidence of injury.

"Drew took a bad fall," said Ned. "He comes to now and again, then slips away."

"Give it to me straight."

Ned hauled in a deep breath. He would have to string together more words now than he ordinarily would utter in a day's time.

"We stopped the train. Drew and Colly boarded the sidewinder. Drew shot and killed the driver. Colly said the driver had a gun and took a shot at Drew, so I guess that's why Drew put him down. Colly took a bullet, but he'll live. He's up in the sidewinder now. Drew told us to board the train. I didn't see it all, but I reckon that feller Torn done all this damage. But your wife had a gun, too."

"What do you mean?"

"I mean she had a gun, and she was ready to use it. The last two cars carried cavalry remounts. Torn stampeded one carload. He and your wife rode south.

"Why didn't you go after them?"

"Only three of us left that could ride. And there were wounded to see to. Had to think about the passengers. We moved 'em all up into the Pullman car. Tanner and Monte are watching over them. We searched 'em for guns and such. Piled the hardware over there in the corner."

Dobson looked at Lute. "Go tell the boys to switch their saddles to those cavalry nags."

As Lute went out the back of the day coach, the Bar ID rider named Monte entered through the front.

"Mr. Dobson. We seen you ride up. So did everybody else in the Pullman. Feller who says he's the conductor wants to palaver."

"He does, does he? I'll do him one better. I'll deal with the whole lot. Ned, bring Drew around. If he can't ride he gets left behind."

When Dobson walked into the Pullman, Monte right behind, the imprisoned passengers raised a clamor. They were packed in tight, and the car was stifling hot. The front door was open. Tanner lounged on the railing of the forward platform, a rifle cradled in his arms.

Dobson drew his sidegun. Shouts of alarm rang out. There was some urgent pushing and shoving. A woman was sobbing, a baby screaming. Dobson fired a round into the roof. That shut down all the noise, except for the infant. Dobson could smell the fear pervading the Pullman.

"My name is Ike Dobson . . ."

"Are you the man in charge?" A squat, pink-faced man in a fine blue broadcloth suit and apricot-orange cravat bulled his way through the tightly packed crowd. "Are you responsible for this . . . this scurrilous banditry? I'll have you know, sir, that you will pay for this outrage. I'll personally see to it." He shook a stubby, well-manicured finger in Dobson's face, spluttering righteous indignation. "I own stock in this railroad, sir. I have an interest in . . ."

Dobson said, "Shut your gate, if you have an interest in staying alive."

The man's eyes dropped to the pistol nudging his well-rounded belly.

"You wouldn't dare," he gasped. He didn't sound too convinced.

"You must not be from these parts, Mr. Boiled Shirt. Else you'd know better than to say that. Now stand back. I want to talk to the conductor, not you."

The man retreated. His place was taken by the Irish train captain.

"I'm the conductor. And I know all about you, Mr. Dobson."

"Good." Dobson holstered the sidegun. "And would you know why this has happened?"

"I'm confused on that score. All I know for certain is that men are dead. Among them, the engineer of this train."

Dobson spoke loudly, so that all could hear.

"I didn't want that. My men were only trying to stop the train. It wasn't a holdup. Your engineer took a shot at my son. He paid the price."

The conductor kept his voice and countenance devoid of emotion. "Your men might have boarded at the Bellefoot station. That way, there would have been no misunderstanding. And the dead would still be among the living."

"My wife was on this train. She's run off with another man. I have a husband's right to bring her back. It's too bad about your compadre. But three of my boys were killed. By the man who stole my wife away from me."

"Buy why are these people being made to suffer? Why are we being held prisoner? Mr. Dobson, we must move this train. Other trains will be coming through."

"Can you ride an iron horse?"

"Aye. I can manage."

"Then take her on to Wichita. But I want one thing understood, and no mistake. I'll be leaving a few of my wounded men on board. They are not to be harmed further. And when you get to Wichita, I want them cared for. If they should come to grief, I'll make damned certain that every soul in that town lives long enough to regret it. And I'll start with you, crum boss."

As he left the Pullman, Dobson snapped off an order to Monte.

"Fetch Tanner. We're burning daylight. I want Torn dead by sunrise."

CHAPTER 13

AFTER THE LAST SHRED OF DAYLIGHT HAD FLED THE western sky, and before the moon rose in the east, Torn and Mary came upon a narrow stream running between steep, grassy banks. Its course was marked by a smattering of cottonwoods and willows.

Torn figured it was as good a place for a brief rest stop as they were likely to find. Their horses needed a breather and water. They took the animals to the stream to drink in moderation, then tied them to a stout cottonwood with tethers long enough to permit grazing, but not so long that they could reach the stream. Torn didn't want the horses waterlogged. Before pressing on, he would take them down to drink once more.

Mary sank to the ground and rested against the trunk of a willow. She was exhausted. Torn hunkered down in front of her.

"How long have you been without food or sleep?" he asked.

She didn't even open her eyes. "I left the ranch last night about this time. At least I had sense enough to wait until after supper. When Ike went into his study to go over the next day's work with his sons and the foreman, Ned Brantley, I stepped out, as though to get a little air. Slipped to the stables without anyone seeing. I had these riding clothes stashed there. And about a hundred dollars in greenbacks. The money was the hardest part. Ike would never let me have any without a strict accounting. I managed to save it up, a little at a time, without his noticing. It took months. But I knew I had to have some, just in case. I've got it in my boot—less the cost of the train fare to Wichita."

"Sounds like your leaving wasn't a spur of the moment thing."

"It wasn't. I kept waiting for a chance—a better chance than the one I took. But it never came. Ike wouldn't let me leave the ranch alone. If I just wanted to take a ride, I had to have one of the hands along."

"He didn't trust you?"

She opened her eyes now. He could see a glimmer of starlight in them. Or maybe it was a glimmer of tears.

"That wasn't it, Mr. Torn. It was because he was afraid that the grangers might try to get back at him by harming me. Ike always expected everyone else to fight in the same dirty and underhanded way he did."

"He had trouble with homesteaders?"

"He *made* trouble for the homesteaders. He wants to drive them away. He hates them for fencing the range and tearing it up with their plows. He says it's his land. He came here first, fought for it, bled for it. When he first started the Bar ID, he only purchased sections along the creeks and rivers. He figured that was all he had to do, since whoever controlled access to the water also controlled the range. That kept other cattlemen away, but not the farmers. A farmer takes a quarter-section, and if it doesn't have running water, he'll dig a well. Most of the Bar ID is really public land, and the farmers have every right to claim it."

Torn nodded. According to the Homestead Act of 1862, a farmer could gain title to a quarter-section after five years' residence. Or, if they could afford it, after six months' residence, they could change their homestead entry to a preemptive entry, pay ten bits an acre, and receive title.

"At first I felt sorry for Ike," she confessed. "He needs hundreds of square miles of graze to maintain his herd, and though he is a powerful man, he's land-poor, like almost every other rancher, and couldn't afford to buy outright all the sections of public land that make up the Bar ID range. But then, as more and more emigrants came in, and more and more claims were made on Bar ID range, Ike got desperate.

"It started with tearing down fences and burning crops. His men would ride at night, on unbranded horses, wearing hoods. The grangers went to the law for protection. Ike bought off the law. Then the grangers banded together to protect themselves. That's when the killing started. The farmers were no match for Ike and his men.

"It was then that I began to see the real Ike Dobson. He didn't fight fair. He fought to win. He's the kind of man who will stop at nothing to get what he wants."

"So I've noticed."

Mary's voice was sharp with bitterness. "His men would ambush farmers in their fields. They went from burning crops to destroying homes. And if the farmer took up his gun to protect his property and family, they'd shoot him down. God, they even shot the women sometimes! And once . . . a farmer's daughter . . . a pretty girl . . . they . . . they . . ."

Off in the tallgrass a red fox barked. The trees danced in the wind. Torn waited until Mary, gazing up at the star-studded sky, had composed herself.

"I tried to make Ike see how terribly, terribly wrong he was. But he became belligerent; sometimes he would hit me. He acted like a cornered animal. I suppose, in a away, he was. His ranch, his dream, was being taken away from him, piece by piece. Finally, I couldn't take any more. I had to leave. I don't know . . . somehow I felt . . . guilty. I didn't destroy anything, or kill anyone, not with my own hands. But I began to think that by being Ike's wife, I was his accomplice."

"You're not to blame, Mary,"

She leaned forward and clutched his sleeve. "I wanted to stop him. Truly, I did. But there was nothing I could do."

"There *is* something you can do. When we get to Wichita, I'll issue a warrant for Ike Dobson's arrest. And you can tell a grand jury what you just told me."

She quickly drew her hand away.

"Are you insane?" she gasped, incredulous.

"He must be stopped. You can help me do it."

"No! I'm going home to my people. I won't help you. You can't make me."

"You're right. I can't make a wife testify against her husband. And I don't *want* to make you do anything against your will. I just thought . . ."

"No! I-I can't."

Torn knew better than to press the issue, realizing suddenly just how afraid Mary was of Ike Dobson. He couldn't blame her. She knew Dobson better than anyone, and if she feared for her life, then there was undoubtedly a good reason for it.

"All right, Mary," he said, hoping to calm her. "I'll help you get home to your people. We'll say no more about it." He rose, and listened for a moment to the prairie night. Taking the pistol he had confiscated on the train from under his belt, he offered it to her. "Why don't you hold onto this until I get back?"

"Get back? Get back from where?" Panic edged her voice.

"Aren't you hungry?"

She laughed—a nervous, tired laugh. "I could eat a horse."

"Afraid we can't spare one of those," he said, deadpan. "And we dare not risk a fire. But maybe I can find something. I won't be gone long, and I won't be far."

She almost asked him to hurry back to her, but caught herself. And as he left her, going upstream, a silent black shadow blending into the dark of night, she wondered at her feelings. Not too long ago, she had taken one look at Clay Torn and decided that she couldn't trust him—that she was better off alone. Now she was convinced that she wouldn't make it without him. She had seen him in action; if there was one man who could protect her from Ike, it was Torn.

Torn moved upstream about fifty yards and found a thicket of wild currant growing under and around the rotting log of a tree that had fallen long ago. It was now midsummer; he discovered an abundance of ripened fruit, and filled his hat with it. Retracing his steps along the soggy edge of the deep and sluggish run, he paused to pull up some bulrushes. Using the saber-knife, he cut a handful of root stalks, rinsed them in the stream, and made his way back toward Mary and the horses.

He pulled up short when he heard a splashing sound ahead. His first thought was that their pursuers had somehow slipped up on them without his knowing, and that Mary was in dire trouble. Dropping his currant-loaded hat and the bulrush roots he began to run, the Colt revolver in hand.

What he saw froze him in his tracks.

Mary's boots, cotton waist and jacket lay on the slope of the bank, and the woman had waded into the stream up to her knees. She had tied the riding skirt up on her thighs with big knots on either hip, and she was naked from the waist up. As he watched, she knelt and splashed water on her face, arms and shoulders. It was dark enough to hide his presence from her, though he stood but twenty feet away.

He knew he ought not to look. But he couldn't help himself.

Torn was captivated by this woman's beauty. He felt the flush of passion—and ruthlessly beat it down. It took a great deal of willpower, almost more than he could muster, to turn away and go back upstream a ways. Finding his hat, he hunkered down on the bank for a moment. He closed his eyes, but he couldn't rid himself of that vivid image. He waited until his heart ceased to pound like a runaway horse in his chest, then gathered up the food and made as much noise as he could, going, *slowly*, back to their camp.

She had the skirt untied and covering her legs, and was fastening the last of the waist's many buttons as he drew near. Torn felt his pulse get quicker as he got closer to her. Her hair was undone and wet, and her clothes clung to damp flesh.

"I couldn't resist," she confessed, with a shy smile. "I had to be rid of the dust and sweat." She sat down in the lush grass to pull on her boots.

Torn set the hatful of currants beside her and knelt to cut open the bulrush roots with his saber-knife.

"Moonrise coming shortly," he declared, thick-tongued. "We'd best be going after we eat this."

She watched him work, mildly amazed. "Somehow, I would never have expected a judge to know about bulrush roots."

He looked up at her, but his eyes were lost in night shadow, and his face seemed cold and hard and dead, reminding her of a skull. She was frightened for a moment, sensing that she had touched a nerve.

"I wasn't always a judge," he replied, and held out a palmful of the tender inner parts of the roots.

Contritely changing the subject, she said, "My people sometimes make flour from these."

"Eat what you can. Then we'll ride."

He left her, climbing to the rim of the bank, breathing deeply to fill his lungs with the sweet night air. The past, with all its bad memories, came rushing up to smother him. He thought back to that time many years ago, in the last weeks of the war, when he had finally escaped Point Lookout Prison. Then, as now, he had been hunted relentlessly by men bent on killing him. He had lived like a hounded animal, running, hiding, trusting no one, a man alone on a dangerous exodus through enemy-occupied territory. Dodging Yankee patrols, he had endured many days and nights with less to sustain him than a handful of edible roots and wild berries. Sheer will had seen him through.

Scanning the dark expanse of prairie, Torn decided that he passionately disliked being the hunted once again.

CHAPTER 14

THEY HAD PUT ONLY A FEW MILES BETWEEN THEM-
selves and the creek when Torn abruptly checked the
mare. It was a move so sharp and unexpected that Mary
cantered right past. She had to turn the sorrel and come
back to him.

"What is it?"

"They're coming."

The fear, by now familiar, came flooding back. She felt
a constriction in her throat. It felt like Ike Dobson had his
rough, iron-fingered hands around her neck and was
squeezing the life out of her. She strained her eyes and
ears, but saw and heard nothing.

"How do you know?" she whispered, hoping against
hope that Torn was mistaken, knowing that he was not
the kind to make such mistakes.

"I know."

He looked with resentment at the three-quarter moon dangling in the eastern sky.

"We're leaving a trail through the tallgrass as wide as the wake of a ship," he told her. "A blind man could follow it in this moonlight."

"I don't see them."

Torn didn't bother trying to explain to her that he didn't see them, either. Or hear them. But he could feel their presence. He had a highly developed and uncanny ability to sense an unseen enemy closing in on him. He knew better than to ignore his instincts.

He kicked the black mare into a gallop. Mary fell in behind.

They covered a couple more miles before stopping again, this time on the west slope of a long and gentle rise. Torn dismounted, handed the mare's rope to Mary, and walked back up to the crest. He waited, squatting with the Winchester across his knees. His gaze incessantly swept the eastern rim of the prairie.

Mary grew impatient. She couldn't understand why they weren't running for all they were worth. The sorrel picked up on her anxiety, and began to pivot and snort. She soothed it with gentle horse talk in her native Muskogee tongue.

Finally Torn saw them. A cluster of black specks spilling over the rim and down a slope, vanishing in a distant fold of the prairie. He judged them to be three miles away. Standing, he looked west. There was no place to hide.

He sorted through the options. They could run, but sooner or later their horses would give out on them. Afoot, they were as good as dead. They could stand and fight, but the odds were too steep. Or he could play the guerrilla game. Lie in wait, ambush them, perhaps even kill one or two and, hopefully, drive them to cover, then ride away until they closed in again, turn, lie in wait, ambush them again . . .

The idea of striking back appealed to Torn. Still, there were many ways for Dobson's men to deal effectively with hit-and-run tactics if Torn chose to employ them. They could split into two groups, and while one group rode under his guns to keep him occupied, the other could pinpoint his location and circle around and in for the kill. There were several ways to skin a cat—or kill the enemy—in a running fight. Torn had learned them all during his years of wartime service.

There was one other way. Lure them off after a decoy and strike out in a totally different direction. With a little luck, he could use the time it would take them to backtrack and pick up his trail to get a long enough head start to stay out of reach until at least moonset.

He went back down the slope to Mary and the horses.

"Get down," he said.

For a panic-stricken moment she thought he was going to abandon her and try to save his own skin. If he left her behind to be captured then he could escape.

But he handed her the rifle, and began to cut swaths in the kneedeep grass with his saber-knife, severing the stalks close to the ground. She realized then that he was still with her—that he had a plan which he thought just might save them.

So she dismounted, and watched as he cut the sorrel's tether rope from around its neck and retied it to the make-shift reins. To the other end of the rope he secured a large, heavy bundle of tallgrass.

"Get a good hold on the mare," he advised, drawing the Colt, and laying it against the sorrel's rump. He thumbed the hammer back and fired. The sorrel bolted away from the searing bite of the crease shot, kicking at the bundle dragging behind it. The mare jumped at the gunshot, almost yanking Mary off her feet.

Torn said, "That should bring them riding full-out. The sorrel ought not to stop this side of the Republican. By the time they catch up to it their horses should be bottomed out."

Holstering the Colt, he swung aboard the mare, helped Mary on behind, and followed in the wake of the sorrel. She looped her arms around him to hold on tight. He felt every inch of her body as it pressed against his. The starlit image of her bathing in the creek tantalized him. He laughed silently at himself. This was a fine time to be thinking about such things!

Faintly, the drumming of hooves reached him. A moment later, he found what he was looking for. The sorrel had charged up a slope and then veered south along the crest, avoiding a particularly steep descent down the far side. Torn guided the mare up the slope in the sorrel's path, then slowly walked the horse down the other side, to the bottom of the hollow. Here he checked the horse, helped Mary down, and dismounted.

Seizing the mare's nose with his right hand, he reached over the animal's neck and grabbed her ear with his left. He wrenched the mare's head savagely. The horse snorted and fought to stay standing. She was strong—which was why Torn had picked her to carry double in the first place. He kicked his legs up and locked them above the mare's withers, twisting her head even more sharply. The mare's legs buckled, and she fell heavily on her side. Torn held her head tightly against his chest.

"Lie down in the grass," he told Mary. "Keep the rifle under your body. Don't want moonlight catching the brass."

"Won't they see us?"

"They'll be looking ahead. Not down here."

"They might see where we branched off."

"Maybe. But they'll be riding hard. If they do see us, I'll let the mare up. And I'll want you on it and riding away as fast as you can."

"What about you?"

"I'll entertain them."

She was too scared to say more. Lying in the tallgrass, the smell of the earth rich and strong in her nostrils, she wondered if she could bring herself to leave this man, if she would make it without him . . .

The thunder of running horses was loud in her ears. She felt the ground shudder beneath the steelshod onslaught. Then the riders appeared, strung out, mounts at a belly-down gallop, looming on the crest of the swell, veering off to the south in the wake of the sorrel. Yes, it would work! With that bundle of tallgrass bouncing to one side and flying off to the other, laying grooves in the prairie carpet, the trail would look enough like that put down by a pair of horses to deceive their pursuers in this less than perfect light.

She could hear the creak of saddle leather, could see their hats and windswept dusters against the moon-silvered sky. How many were there? Fifteen? Twenty? More? Would the procession never end? All it would take was one sharp-eyed rider, glancing down into the hollow. The night shadows were deeper here—but were they deep enough?

Suddenly, they were gone. The hoofbeats faded. Mary's entire body tingled with the dizzy exultation of relief. She saw Torn let the mare up, and couldn't resist stepping over to put her arms around him and hug him jubilantly.

"We're going to make it." she laughed. "I know it now."

Torn was surprised, but he didn't break away from her.

Not this time. A man just had so much willpower when it came to such things. He held her, tentatively.

"You can win all the battles, Mary," he allowed soberly, "and still lose the war."

CHAPTER

15

MARY WOKE AT FIRST LIGHT. SHE HEARD BOBWHITE quail greeting the dawn, and guessed that this was what had brought her from the depths of an exhausted sleep. After they had eluded the Bar ID pursuit, much of the tension had gone out of her, replaced by utter fatigue. Long after moonset, Torn had stopped to let her benefit from a few hours' sleep.

Sitting up, she found the mare standing beside her, cropping grass with its blunt teeth. The neck rope was fastened around her waist. Mary couldn't remember taking this precaution herself, and assumed that Torn was responsible. Standing, she untied the rope, and winced at the complaint of stiff joints and sore muscles as she bent to retrieve the pistol Torn had given her, tucking it beneath the belt that held the riding skirt at her narrow waist.

She saw that she stood on low ground, while Torn was sitting on the crest of a rise to the east, his back to her.

She climbed to join him, leading the mare, trying to brush off her clothes and work the grass burrs out of her hopelessly tangled hair. For some reason she wanted to look as presentable as possible for Torn.

"Did you get any rest?" she asked as she sat beside him, gazing in wonder at the pink and rose panorama of dawn colors in the eastern sky. Strips of high cirrus clouds radiated like wheel spokes across the lightening sky, and the strongest stars flickered weakly in a hopeless struggle against extinction. Even the prairie wind had stilled momentarily, as though calmed by the gentle touch of morning.

"I'll rest later," he said, and pointed to the southwest. "Look there."

She saw the column of black smoke tilting into the sky.

"What is it?"

"Smoke."

"Oh, you!" she scolded with a laugh. "There you go again."

"I don't know what it's coming from," he said soberly. "But we'd do well to find out. If your husband has anything to do with it, we ought to know."

Mention of Dobson took all the morning freshness and enthusiasm right out of her.

"I just want to go home," she murmured, her voice dull.

Torn rose and mounted, holding out a hand to help her mount the mare. She took it reluctantly and got on behind him. He kicked the horse into its natural gait, making for the smoke.

The previous night's ride had convinced Torn that his hasty selection of the black mare had been a stroke of luck. She was a well-muscled and well-mannered animal with a smooth square gait and great stamina. They had gone many miles and twelve hours since the last drink, and the mare still had a spring in her step.

They cut the trail of their pursuers, and Torn followed it to the next rise, where, he noticed, Dobson's men had fanned out and paused before descending at the gallop. Down below, the prairie flattened out. Dead center of this level stretch was a small sod house. Beyond it was a cultivated field—or what was left of it. The crop had been destroyed, for it was here that the fire had started. The flames had spread to damage the soddy, consume a picket cow shed and drift into the tallgrass to the west and south. Torn saw the body of a man sprawled in front of the soddy, and the carcass of a cow further out.

A woman and young girl were running back and forth between the well and the house, dousing the soddy with water carried in buckets. A soddy was not impervious to fire; the wooden frames of the door and a pair of windows were still burning. Some of the viga roof beams had burned as well, and sections of the roof had collapsed.

"Yes," said Mary bitterly. "It looks like my husband has been here. Fire and death, those are his calling cards."

Torn shook his head grimly. He was of the opinion that the Bar ID riders who followed Dobson were not really bonafide hardcases—despite all the evidence to the contrary. No, more likely they were average cowpunchers compelled to step over the line of civilized behavior by their blind obedience to Dobson. He had seen something like this in the war. Decent men driven to barbarous acts. He had seen it again in the actions of vigilante mobs on the frontier. It was the sort of thing that reminded him— a man who needed no reminding—that civilization was only a thin veneer, and that men were animals when cut to the quick.

He kicked the mare into a hard gallop down the slope.

They were halfway to the soddy when the woman saw them coming. She threw down her bucket and ran to the body of the dead man, who lay face down across a double-barreled shotgun. She pulled the weapon free and brought it to bear. Torn checked the mare twenty yards shy of her.

"Go away!" warned the woman hoarsely. "Go away or by God I'll shoot."

As the day aged the wind had picked up again—that ever present zephyr relentlessly scouring the prairie, that could drive men mad with its endless banshee wail, and that now propelled the ever-widening fire across the valley. It threw the smoke from the ruined field and charred buildings in choking drifts that were level with the ground, and Torn narrowed his eyes against its sting as he looked steadily down the twin barrels of the 12-gauge scattergun.

"We've come to help," he said.

"You're too late." The woman glanced at the dead man. The shotgun lowered, and she swayed, perilously close to fainting. But she caught herself, and her chin rose, and she lifted her soul out of despair and grief.

Torn dismounted, handing Mary the Winchester and the reins of Manila hemp, and went up to the woman. She was tall and big-boned. Her long face was covered with soot streaked with sweat or tears, or both. Sunwashed eyes were red and swollen from the smoke's bite. She was barefoot. Her hands were rough and scarred, the fingernails dirty and cracked. There were holes in her much-mended brown gingham dress where wind-carried embers had burned the fabric. But for all that, she was in Torn's eyes a fine-looking woman, with her head held high, an indomitable spirit unbroken by this flood of calamity. She looked forty; taking into account the unending hardships a pioneer wife endured, he figured she was not, in fact, much past twenty-five.

He took the shotgun from her, put the hammers down, and cast it aside.

"It's too late for *that*," he said, and brushed past her to the little girl. Perhaps seven summers old, the child was stumbling past them towards the soddy, struggling to carry a bucket of water, staggering under the burden and sloshing half the contents along the way. Torn reached down and grasped the pail. She looked up at him, her face blank with shock and exhaustion.

"I'll take over for you, darlin'," he said gently.

She relinquished the bucket, stepped back, and plopped limply down onto the scorched earth. Torn carried the bucket into the soddy, threw the water on the nearest smoldering roofpole and came out coughing. The soddy was filled with swirling smoke. He almost collided with the black mare and looked up at Mary.

"I want to help," she said.

"Keep hauling water out of that well, then."

She spun the black around and rode to the well. When Torn reached her, she had tied the mare to one of the uprights of the hoisting frame and was working the windlass crank to elevate the bucket. A glance at the rope on the windlass told Torn that the well was at least forty feet deep. Forty feet—it had been excavated with pick and shovel and gallons of sweat by the farmer lying dead over there. The hoisting frame itself had been fashioned from stout white oak lumber cannibalized from a Conestoga wagon—the same wood that had been used to frame the windows and door of the soddy, as well as the door itself, which had now burned and fallen from its leather hinges. As he carried a bucket of water back to the house, Torn thought about all the backbreaking work that had been put into this homestead, and the more he thought about it, the angrier he became.

They worked for almost an hour, Torn and the pioneer woman hauling water from the well, Mary throwing the iron-bound wellbucket down and cranking it back up. Mary worked like a woman possessed. She never made the others wait long for water. Ignoring the red-hot pain lancing through her arms and shoulders, she pushed herself to the limit and beyond. She lost track of how many times she raised the wellbucket. The well seemed to get deeper and the water heavier, and her breath rasped in her throat, but she kept on, fiercely. In a small way she was fighting back at Ike Dobson, and it felt right.

She was blind with fatigue, but still cranking, when Torn reached in to grab the windlass handle and stop her.

"We've done all we can do," he told her.

She let go of the crank. The bucket plummeted and splashed. She looked at her abraded hands, and shook her head.

"No, it's not all. I can do more. Ike has got to be stopped. He's gone mad. I'll help you stop him."

"You're the one," said the other woman, behind them.

They turned to face the new-made widow.

"The man leading them that done this—a big man, with a face like a stone and a voice like thunder—he said he was after his wife who run away. And the man she run away with."

"I'm so sorry . . ." Mary's voice cracked, and a solitary tear slipped down her cheek.

The woman continued, her voice hollow as she recited tragedy. She stood, barefoot on the blackened earth, her dress hanging in tatters on her gaunt frame.

"Last night, we heard a horse. My husband come out to find a sorrel wearin' a rope, and the rope had caught up in the fence yonder. And then the riders come at first light. My husband said he hadn't seen the two of you, but the big man called him a liar, on account he saw the sorrel. They searched everywhere, tore up the house and all in it. Then they set fire to the spring wheat. The big man said you might be hidin' in it, but that was an excuse. You could see that in his face. When they shot the cow, my husband fetched his gun. They gunned him down and rode off. They took the sorrel horse. The fire spread fast. Too fast. The wind blew it straight at the house. I didn't know what else to do but take little Julie down into the root cellar. The smoke was everywhere, and I couldn't be sure which way to run, and besides, the fire was spreading faster than a body *could* run."

Torn looked to the west and south. The fire was racing through the tallgrass, a thin line of flame not much taller than a man in most places. It was already a mile wide, and still spreading. Nothing but strong rain or a wide river would stop it. A day or a week, maybe even more—there was no way of knowing how long it would burn.

"Which way did they ride out?" he asked.

"They split up. One bunch went north, the other toward the sunrise."

Torn nodded. Ike still hoped to cut their trail. Giving up was not in Ike Dobson.

The woman, half-staggering, stepped in close to Mary. Torn watched her warily, wondering if she intended to strike out. Mary had the same thought, but she stood her ground, like a repentant child accepting just punishment.

But the woman reached out and with a trembling finger brushed the tear from Mary's cheek.

"Tears won't do no good. From what I seen, I can't fault you for leaving your husband. It was just our bad luck we was in the big man's way. It ain't the first bad luck we've had. Won't be the last."

Mary almost broke down. The woman's charity was harder to take than the wrath she had expected.

"What will you do?" she asked.

The woman scanned the destruction that lay all about them, and squared her shoulders.

"Start over, I reckon. Bury my husband, and commence to start from scratch."

"But you can't . . . you can't stay out here alone . . ."

"Who says I can't?" snapped the woman defiantly. "I can plow and plant, good as any man. Come fall, I'll plant winter wheat, if I can get seed. Till then I'll hunt food for the table. I'm a fair shot."

Mary bent down, took a roll of greenbacks from her boot, and offered it to the woman.

"Take it. Please. It's not much. Almost a hundred dollars. Buy your seed, and . . ."

"I can't take your money."

"It's not my money. I stole it from my husband. The big man. It's his money. It's only right that he pay for the damage he's done."

The woman thought it over, staring at the paper money held out to her. It was, Torn was sure, more money than she had ever seen.

"Yes, I reckon it's right," she nodded, and, much to Mary's relief, took the money.

"That's not all Ike Dobson will pay," promised Mary fiercely. "That's just the beginning. He'll pay much more dearly before I'm through."

Torn said, "I'll help you bury your husband, ma'am."

"No, I'druther. You folks go on. It ain't safe for you here. They might circle back. You can't never tell which way an ill wind will blow."

Moments later, Torn and Mary were astride the black mare and riding west. At the crest of the first rise, Torn felt her turn and look back.

"I hate to think of them alone way out here," she said.

"If I had to choose between that woman and the prairie," said Torn, "I'd put my money on the woman."

CHAPTER

16

TORN USED THE NIGHT SHADOWS TO GOOD ADVAN-
tage as he worked his way through the rows of freight
cars and empty passenger coaches that stood in the A, T
& SF railyard on the south edge of Wichita. Cattle bawled
from the vast stockyards to his right. Dimly, from the less
than respectable south side of town, he could hear the
plinking of a piano, and a quick staccato volley of male
laughter. He stopped once, crouching, as the yardmaster
trudged past on the other side of a line of boxcars, his
heavy boots crunching in the gravel. The man was carrying
a lighted lantern, and singing the popular hymn "Washed
in Blood" in a rich baritone. Torn waited until the railroader
was well past before moving on.

The Wichita depot was a palace in comparison to the
renovated boxcar that served Pitchfork Slough. A long
structure with a steep green tile roof, it boasted a platform
as long as a short train, and wide galleries on the east and

west. There were wood and wrought-iron benches on the galleries, and lighted storm lanterns bracketed to shiplap walls.

The telegraph office, open day and night, had a window facing out onto the west gallery. Torn saw a man wearing a green eyeshade sitting inside. He circled, cat-footed, outside the throw of light from the lanterns and mounted the empty platform, entering the depot through a pair of tall, glass-inset doors, pausing briefly to scan the schedule board on the wall beside the entrance. As he stepped inside, the big Elgin wall clock behind the ticket counter chimed the half hour.

The depot was empty, as Torn had expected at half past midnight. The next train, an emigrant run, was not due for hours; the eastbound flyer from the Colorado end-of-line had passed an hour earlier. The big, high-ceilinged room with its rows of columns and ranks of benches was as quiet as a church on Monday morning.

Torn moved to the counter on the balls of his feet. A station agent, young and wearing spectacles as thick as bottle glass, sat on a stool reading a Beadle dime novel. He was so engrossed in the tall tale that Torn stood at the counter unnoticed for a full minute. When Torn tapped his knuckles lightly on the counter top, the agent almost fell off his perch.

"Quiet night," observed Torn.

"*Too* quiet," vouched the agent.

"Didn't mean to startle you."

The young man laughed nervously. "I admit, I'm as edgy as a rabbit in a coyote's back pocket. You would be, too, if you were sharing your quarters with three dead bodies."

Torn looked around. "Three dead bodies?"

The agent pointed with his chin. "Over in the baggage room."

"What happened?"

"You been away? I thought everybody heard the news. There was big trouble on the railroad yesterday—well, I guess it was the day before yesterday, now. Men who work for Ike Dobson stopped the train. The engineer thought it was a holdup. It wasn't, though. They were just trying to find Mr. Dobson's wife." The agent leaned forward, pitching his voice to a conspiratorial whisper. "Word has it she run off with another man. What do you think about that?"

"Not much," said Torn stiffly.

"Well, like I said, the engineer thought it was a holdup, and started shooting. He sure milked the wrong cow that time, 'cause he got killed for it. So did the fireman. Apparently tried to jump off the train and broke his neck. Those three in there are Dobson men. Shot by the feller who took off with Dobson's wife. We're waiting to see if Dobson's going to come claim the bodies. If he isn't here by tomorrow I suppose they'll be buried in our local bone orchard. I sure hope so. Gives me the bejabbers, being all night around dead men."

"When I kill a man," said Torn, "he generally stays dead."

At first the agent stared blankly; then all the color drained out of his face as he felt the full implications of Torn's flat-delivered statement.

"Oh my God..."

"The way you tell it wasn't exactly the way it happened," said Torn drily. "But, be that as it may, I had to quit that train right quick, and so left some of my belongings behind. Including a clean shirt and pair of pants, which, as you can see, I'm in strong need of."

The agent looked at Torn's soiled attire, his Adam's apple bobbing in his throat.

"Why, you just feel free to help yourself, sir," urged the agent, with the utmost servility. "Baggage room's through that door over there."

"You come along with me."

"Oh, no sir! I mean, I'd rather not, what with three corpses and all . . ."

"You *will* come along with me."

One look into Torn's steel-gray eyes, and the agent knew he didn't have a choice.

"Well, if you insist."

They crossed the waiting room, Torn staying a little behind and to one side of the agent, half-expecting the railroad employee to bolt. He didn't, though, and they entered the depot baggage room, Torn gesturing for the agent to precede him.

Silver threads of moonlight came through the barred windows across the room. There were long tables on either side, and Torn saw his saddle under one of them, but then he heard a noise and swung his gaze towards the window. The three pine coffins were stacked, one on top of the other two, beneath the window.

"There's a lamp over . . ." began the agent.

"Shut up."

Torn saw movement over near the coffins. So did the agent. As the latter shrieked and jumped backward, Torn pounced to the right, sweeping the frock coat back and the Colt out of its holster in one smooth, quicker-than-the-eye movement.

"Lay off the trigger," came a dead-calm voice. "And somebody fire up a lamp."

Torn glanced left. The agent lay in a motionless heap on the floor. He had fainted. Torn straightened, and put the Peacemaker away. He had recognized the voice.

"Stay put a minute, Wyatt," he advised, with a dose of

sarcasm. "Wouldn't want you to fall over something and hurt yourself."

"That's mighty white of you, Clay."

Torn fished a black metal match case out of his coat pocket, extracted a "strike-anywhere," and in a moment had the wall lamp burning. He turned to find Wyatt Earp sitting on one of the bottom coffins, leaning back against the topmost.

"What happened to him?" asked Wyatt, nodding at the agent.

"You scared him."

"Huh!" Wyatt looked puzzled, like he didn't know the meaning of the word scared. "Been waiting on you, Clay, Figured you'd come for your possibles, sooner or later. Guess I dozed off. Wish it had been sooner. These fellers are beginning to sour."

Torn smiled grimly. Stretching out for a little shut-eye on the coffins of a trio of day-old dead men—yes, that sounded like the Wyatt Earp he knew.

"Sorry I made you wait, Wyatt. Hope it wasn't anything urgent."

"But it was. Still is," Wyatt stood, stretched, and strolled closer, thumbs hooked behind the buckle of his gunbelt. He wore a tailored black suit and vest, of fine quality, and expensive handlasted boots—better garb, thought Torn, than one might expect to find on a man making forty dollars a month, the wages of a deputy town marshal.

Wyatt was a wide-shouldered man with a jutting jaw, piercing blue eyes and a sweeping tawny mustache. Torn had met him on several occasions, and knew something about him. One of five brothers, he had tried his hand as a teamster in Arizona Territory and a section hand with the Union Pacific in Wyoming before finding his true calling as a gambler. More recently, he had been suspected of horse-stealing in the Nations. These days he was one of Marshal Meagher's deputies. It was rumored that he pocketed most of the fines he collected and operated a protection racket that cost many of Wichita's cribhouses and watering holes a pretty penny. His allegiance was to profit, not law and order. He was a good man to have on your side, mused Torn, if you could afford him, because Wyatt Earp, for all his shortcomings in the scruples department, was a fearless fighter and a lethal hand with a gun. Of course, he was also the last man you wanted for an enemy.

"You've been raising a lot of dust, Clay," said Wyatt affably. "Judge Stephens wants to see you, pronto. He says to bring you, whether you want to go or not, whatever the hour. As is his custom on Thursday nights, he is at the Hotel Carey barroom, in an all-night poker game. Which is where I should be, come to think of it. Now, I know you're a federally appointed judge, and Judge Stephens is just an elected local official, but the fact is, it's the locals who pay my salary. So I hope you'll consent to coming along peaceably, Clay."

"I'll go, Wyatt. Truth be known, I was planning to pay a call on Judge Stephens anyway. After I spruced up a bit."

"You look fine, Clay, for a man with an acre of Kansas dust on his clothes. How long have you been in town?"

"A few hours."

"How come you've taken to sneaking around in the middle of the night like a thief?"

"Have a care, Wyatt."

"Sorry, Clay. No offense meant."

"None taken."

"By the way, where's Mrs. Dobson?"

"Safe."

It was curtly spoken. Wyatt Earp could tell that Torn had no intention of elaborating. Looking at Torn, realized Earp, was like looking in a mirror. He saw a hard man with cold eyes and a quick gunhand.

Wyatt shrugged. "My orders are to bring you in. Not to find her."

"I'm awfully glad to hear that," said Torn. "Because it means we can keep this friendly."

C H A P T E R

17

THE HOTEL CAREY WAS WICHITA'S MOST POSH HOS-
telry. Its barroom was a showplace. The bar was ornately
carved mahogany resting on a base of white marble. On
the wall behind the bar was a wide pier glass. Neatly
stacked ranks of bottles stood in high cabinets on either
side of the mirror. The walls were covered with green
damask.

There was one bartender on duty, to serve the needs
of the four men playing poker at a corner table. At this
late hour, they were the only patrons. Torn knew all four
of them by sight.

State District Judge R.G. Stephens was a bald, round-
bellied man with a florid complexion. Torn thought, un-
charitably, that Stephens looked like a man who had lived
so high on the hog for so long that he was beginning to
resemble one. He was a shrewd man with political aspi-

rations, and he wasn't above using his position to further those goals.

Wichita's town marshal, Michael Meagher, was a swarthy, black-haired character who, like Stephens, took a self-serving approach to his job. To his right sat a gaunt, hawk-nosed gentleman in a brown tweed suit. J. Benedict Hambacher was the district manager of the A, T & SF Railroad. Hambacher looked pleasantly mild-mannered, but he had a well-deserved reputation as a hard-as-nails businessman, a real power in Kansas. He answered only to the railroad's president, Cyrus Holliday.

The presence of the fourth man surprised Torn. It was the cardsharp he had thrown off the train at Pitchfork Slough.

Dice Fontane felt uneasy as he watched Torn stride to the corner table, Wyatt Earp in tow. His smile tightened. He nervously fingered his pencil-thin mustache. Torn did not fail to notice the gambler's right hand slipping out of sight beneath the table.

"Well, Wyatt," said Meagher, "you got him, I see. Good work."

"I didn't *get* him," corrected Wyatt icily. He was not fond of Meagher, and had his sights set on the marshal's job. Sitting down to a gentleman's game over bonded whiskey and imported cigars with powerful men—that was where Wyatt Earp wanted to be.

Stephens threw down his hand and scowled, disgusted, at Torn.

"Sir, you have caused a great stir. What do you have to say for yourself?"

"I'm issuing a federal warrant for the arrest of Ike Dobson. As a courtesy, I thought I should tell you."

Stephens stared, slack-jawed. Meagher knocked back a

shot of Scotch. Hambacher seemed amused, as though he thought Torn had cracked a good joke.

"What did you say?" asked Stephens, incredulous.

"You heard me."

"On what charge?" challenged Meagher.

"Assault with intent to commit a felony. Attempted kidnapping. Conspiracy to commit murder. Will that do for a start?"

"A complaint must be lodged before a judge can issue a warrant," said Stephens stiffly.

"I have a complainant."

"Now, Judge Torn," said Hambacher, his tone silky. "Let's conduct ourselves like reasonable gentlemen. There has been a grave misunderstanding that resulted in tragic deaths. Let's not compound the problem."

It was Torn's turn to be incredulous. "Ike Dobson's men stopped and boarded one of your trains, Mr. Hambacher. They put your passengers at risk. There are plenty of witnesses to that fact, starting with the train crew and the Pitchfork Slough station agent."

Hambacher cleared his throat. "Mr. Schuyler, the station agent, was found shot to death. We don't know what happened because there is no one left in Pitchfork Slough. In fact, the town was burned to the ground."

"We all know what happened."

"The engineer and the fireman on that train were killed."

"I'll have to tack on a charge of murder."

"Murder?" yelped Stephens. "From what we heard, it was self-defense."

"Who sold you that bill of goods?"

"There might be a warrant issued for your arrest, Judge," said Meagher, pouring himself another shot of Scotch. "A couple of Bar ID men came in on that train. Wounded men. Along with three dead ones. They say you killed those three. They claim they were just trying to get Mrs. Dobson back. That she'd run off. The engineer was killed when he fired on them. And this gentleman here— " Meagher nodded at Fontane "—says Mrs. Dobson was running off with you."

"You've got several facts wrong, Marshal," said Torn, glaring at Fontane. "For one thing, this man is no gentleman. Of course, if he doesn't put his hand back on the table where I can see it, what kind of man he is won't matter anymore."

Fontane, rigid in his chair, slowly put his hands flat on the table. His coyote eyes shot daggers of hate at Torn.

"You took my gun, remember? When you assaulted me and threw me off that train."

"And like a bad penny, you just keep turning up."

"Did you kill those three cowboys?" asked Stephens.

"I did." Torn fastened steel-cast eyes on Meagher. "Going to arrest me, Marshal?"

There was a deadly challenge in that query that sent a cold chill up Meagher's spine.

"No one's sworn out a complaint, yet." Meagher looked at Judge Stephens. "Or issued a warrant." He kicked back another shot of courage.

"Do you deny being in the company of Ike Dobson's wife?" asked Stephens.

"No. I don't deny it."

Stephens resumed his seat with the smug, self-satisfied expression of one who has made his point with telling impact.

"Well then, sir, let me ask you another question. Do you know the term 'alienation of affections'? A serious offense. The willful and malicious interference with a marriage relationship by a third party."

"Without justification or excuse," amended Torn. "Both

of which I have. Mary Dobson can testify to the fact that her husband has waged war on homesteading families. His men have burned crops and homes. They have terrorized and violated women. They have gunned down farmers in cold blood."

"Those are serious allegations," warned Stephens. "Did Mrs. Dobson see all this with her own eyes?"

"I did. Yesterday, Dobson and his men hit a homestead not twenty miles east of here. They put it to the torch and killed the farmer, leaving a woman and a young child to fend for themselves."

"Now why would Mr. Dobson do such a thing?"

"You know why. You all do. And all of you can look the other way if you choose to. But I won't." He looked at Hambacher. "What about the railroad?"

"It was an unfortunate misunderstanding," said Hambacher flatly, no longer in the mood for pretense. "We intend to let the matter drop."

"You lay down with the dogs, you get up with fleas," muttered Torn.

"This is outrageous!" yelped Stephens, his face beet red. "You are an unreconstructed rebel, Mr. Torn! I'd like to know how you got to be a federal judge in the first place."

"Lucky, I guess."

"We don't want trouble in Wichita," said Meagher. "I figure Ike Dobson will ride in here himself any time now. He'll be coming for his dead and wounded. And for his wife. I intend to see that he gets everything he comes for."

"You'll also have in hand a warrant for his arrest."

"This is not your jurisdiction," protested Stephens. "If there are any warrants to be issued, I'll issue them. I tell you what, Judge Torn. Bring Mrs. Dobson to me. I'll hear what she has to say."

Torn dismissed this ploy without wasting words.

"Dobson's crimes were committed on public lands given to farmers in accordance with an act of Congress." He glared at Hambacher. "And on a railroad subsidized by the federal government and operating on property that was given by a Congressional land grant."

"You can issue warrants until you're blue in the face," said Meagher. "But you better find a federal marshal to serve them. I sure as hell won't."

"I didn't expect you to. Besides, I reserve that pleasure for myself."

"He'll kill you," said Fontane, obviously relishing the prospect. "And maybe I'll be there, so that I can testify it was self-defense."

Torn's smile was bleak. "Don't stand too close to him. You might catch a bullet."

CHAPTER 18

"YOU CAN'T BLAME THEM," SAID TED JUDAH, FILL-ing Torn's just-emptied shot glass with Overholt bourbon.

"Sure I can," replied Torn.

"Here, drown your sorrows with a bit more of this bobwire extract. Clay, you can't expect everyone to live by your rigid standards."

Torn drank half the bourbon. "Sure I can."

Judah rolled a cigar in his teeth, grinning at Torn. He was a big bear of a man with a thick black beard and a jolly demeanor.

"If you want to know where a man is coming from, you need to know where he's going."

Torn glared skeptically. Judah could sense his seething anger. They were sitting at Judah's private table, at the rear of the Lady Gay Saloon on Market Street. At this late hour, the watering hole was closed for the night. A barkeep was toweling glasses behind the bar, and a swamper was cleaning up behind the hash counter. Judah had been counting up the day's take when Torn arrived. The table was strewn with greenbacks and hard money, and a metal strongbox sat at the saloon owner's elbow.

"I think you've got that backwards," said Torn.

"Not in this case. Those men are concerned most of all with their futures. And no one concerned with his future stands in Ike Dobson's way."

"How come you know so much?"

"I make it a habit to know everything about everybody. For instance, I know that Ike Dobson and the governor of this state are close friends. You can bet that Judge Stephens and Mr. Hambacher know that, too. Now, the last thing that the railroad wants is trouble with Dobson."

"Dobson's men killed two trainmen and a station agent."

"And they don't want to lose any more employees. It's bad for business. There was a time, in the not too distant past, when Ike Dobson was the only law in this neck of the woods. He's always had to fight to hold on to what he has. He's done it with gun and grit, and he's too old a dog to learn new tricks."

"Sounds like you're making excuses for him."

"Not at all. I'm just telling you that Stephens and Hambacher are sensible men with a keen sense of self-preservation, who know better than to climb into a pen with a bull on the prod. It's not that they don't want Dobson stopped. They just don't want to pay what it's going to cost to stop him."

"Fact is," said Torn, "that the old saying about absolute power corrupting absolutely is true. I've seen it before."

Judah nodded. "Yes, I remember your telling me about Karl Schmidt."

Judah was one of the few men who knew the whole story. Torn had told him some time ago, when Judah had first inquired about the saber-knife Torn carried in that shoulder harness, under his coat. The saloon owner appreciated the fact that Torn had seen fit to confide in him. And he had seen then, as he saw now, that the memory was a grim one for Torn.

Karl Schmidt had been a Union sergeant, and head guard at Point Lookout Prison, where Torn had spent the last year-and-a-half of the late war. He had also been a sadist, a man who derived immense satisfaction from the suffering he caused the Confederate prisoners languishing in that Maryland hellhole. Clay Torn, proud and unbroken by the hardships of captivity, had become a target for much of Schmidt's brutality. But no matter how much he beat and bullied Torn, Schmidt couldn't break him. And one day he had made a careless fatal mistake, and Torn had seized his sword and ripped the sergeant from sternum to scrotum.

Torn had escaped Point Lookout—to stay would have meant certain death. Armed only with Schmidt's saber, he had somehow managed to work his way back to South Carolina, arriving to find the war lost, and his home and family destroyed.

It was small wonder, mused Judah, that Torn had set his sights on Ike Dobson. Any man who abused his power and position and rode roughshod over innocent or helpless people was likely to remind Torn of Karl Schmidt—much to the other man's detriment.

"Look, Clay," said Judah, "I'm not on Dobson's side. But there's that adage from the Bible, about knowing thine enemy, that I think you should heed."

"I know all I need to know," said Torn adamantly.

"Do you? Tell me, how did you feel when you got back home to South Carolina and found your family estate ransacked by Sherman's boys, all the fine things stolen? And later, when the carpetbaggers came and took the land piece by piece, what were your feelings then?"

"There wasn't a lot I could do at the time. I was a wanted man. Wanted for Schmidt's murder. I spent my time dodging Yankee patrols and scalawag posses. By the time the amnesty came through, the deed was done. There wasn't anything left to fight over. Besides, I was more interested in finding Melony."

"Oh, yes. Melony. If you had found the men who took her, would you have killed them?"

"I know what you're trying to say. But that was different. Melony didn't leave of her own free will. She was abducted. The same cannot be said in Mary Dobson's case. Ike has no right to hold her against her will."

"I can understand how you'd feel strongly about that, after sixteen months in a Federal prison camp."

"And as to the Torn estate, you have to remember that the Federal army, at the end of the war, either emptied all the courthouses of the pertinent documents, or burned them to the ground. That included all the land titles. I couldn't have proven that the land belonged to my family had I even tried. Which, of course, was the purpose of the policy to remove or destroy those documents in the first place."

"Then you should know how Dobson feels. He almost single-handedly opened up this country hereabouts. He didn't have the money to buy all the land he needed, but he took possession of it at a time when nobody but the Indians had the slightest interest in it. I suspect he feels as though he deserves to keep it—that possession is nine-tenths of the law."

Torn almost smiled. "Funny. I once expressed that same opinion to Mary Dobson."

"Dobson lost his first wife and a brother to this land.

Now he's losing the land itself. And Mary. I don't condone his actions, but I'm not surprised by them, either."

Torn nodded. He knew that Judah wasn't really trying to build a defense for Dobson. The saloon owner simply liked to play devil's advocate. He was known as a man who took no sides on an issue, and while he was not generally trusted, neither was he often involved in conflicts. This allowed Judah to negotiate disputes between warring factions in Wichita, on occasion.

"You say you know everything about everybody," said Torn.

Grinning, Judah spread his hands. "I can't stand false modesty. Can you?"

"Mary—Mrs. Dobson—said Ike has two sons..."

"Drew and Lute. And you know, now that you mention it, there's something about those two that you should know. Word has it that they don't much care for their stepmother. That they'd sooner see her dead than back home. They don't want to share their inheritance with anyone, especially with an Indian. It was Indians that killed their real mother. Kiowa, back in '62, if memory serves."

"That didn't seem to bother Ike."

"Story is that Dobson met Mary at the depot restaurant in Topeka. I guess it was a case of pretty winning over prejudice. What brought her there... well, I'm afraid I don't know for certain. But a lot of young women from the Five Civilized Tribes leave the Nations, looking for something better than working in the fields."

"I never thought I'd hear you say you didn't know something."

"I also don't know where Mary Dobson is at this very moment," said Judah, "and I don't want to know. But I am a little curious as to why you're in no apparent hurry to get back to your star witness against Dobson."

"I was followed from the Hotel Carey."

"Really? By who?"

"I don't know. I didn't see anybody. But I felt them."

"What are you going to do about it?"

"I have a couple of ideas."

"They might be left with the impression that she is hidden here."

Torn gave his friend a hard look. "That occurred to me. I was hoping you wouldn't mind helping out a little. But I didn't have the chance to ask first."

Judah chuckled, a deep rumble like distant thunder. "I don't mind a little excitement, if it's for a good cause." He picked up the bottle of Overholt. "Another dose of nose paint, Judge?"

Torn covered the glass with his hand. "It pains me to decline such a generous offer, since this is one of the few places in Kansas where I can get honest-to-God bourbon."

"And on the house, too."

"But now's hardly the time to get hymn-singing drunk." He took the daguerreotype from his coat pocket. "If you remember, you sent word to me . . ."

"I was wondering when we'd get around to that. Here, let me see that again." Gravely studying the image of Melony Hancock, Judah nodded. "There *is* a resemblance, but I can't say for certain, Clay. I'm sorry. Besides, this was taken, what, over fifteen years ago? Your Melony will have changed some in that length of time, I imagine."

"Where did you see the woman?"

Judah put the daguerreotype gently on the table and sat back in his chair, no longer looking jolly.

"She works on the line."

Torn's expression was bleak. He recovered the daguerreotype and returned it to his pocket. It was something he always lived with: the possibility that Melony had been changed for the worse by her experiences, and obliged to lower herself in order to survive. And he knew, if this turned out to be the case, that he would feel responsible. It wasn't reasonable, he knew, to assume the burden of guilt for riding off to some foolish war and leaving his fiancée to her fate, but Torn carried that burden nonetheless. Until he found Melony, he would always carry it.

"If it is her," said Judah, feeling sorry for Torn, "and if I were in your boots, I'd try to keep in mind that out here people do what they have to in order to survive."

Torn drew a long breath. "Thanks, Ted. I'll check it out tomorrow."

"I saw her north of Douglas, where she wasn't supposed to be. I followed her—tried to get closer—but she must've thought I was John Law, for she headed back to the line, double-quick. She disappeared on me, but I think she works on the east end, by the river."

Torn nodded. "I'd better be going."

"What about the man, or men, following you? I wouldn't put it past Meagher, or even Judge Stephens, to try and take Mrs. Dobson away from you before Ike arrives. They're probably afraid he'll tear Wichita right down to the ground to find her. Of course, neither one has the gumption to do it himself, but there are plenty of hardcases in this town who'll slit your throat for a silver dollar."

"Like I said, I have an idea." And Torn gave his friend the details.

A minute later Judah was calling the bartender over to the table.

"Frank, Judge Torn here has a job for you, if you'll take it."

"I'm listening."

"Somebody—maybe one man, maybe more—followed me here. I figure they're still waiting outside. They're hoping I'll lead them to someone else. I need a volunteer, a man my size, to go out that door wearing my coat and hat."

"A decoy," murmured Frank.

"That's right. Hopefully whoever it is will follow you, and I'll come in on them from behind."

Frank glanced at Judah. "You want me to do this, Mr. Judah?"

"I won't tell you to. We can't guarantee that your life won't be at risk. But, if I was of the proper build—" Judah ruefully patted his sides "—I'd take the job myself."

Frank nodded. He showed no more emotion than a stone-faced Apache bronco. "Then I reckon I'll go along."

"Good," said Torn. "It's possible that they're watching us right now through the windows. So I suggest you go back to the storeroom, and I'll follow in a minute. Then you'll take my hat and coat, come out, leave through the front door, and walk south."

Without another word, Frank turned and went through the door at the rear of the saloon.

"You haven't nailed down that floor hatch back there, have you, Ted?"

"It's right where it's always been."

Torn stood. "Thanks for everything."

"Take care of Frank, now. Good aprons are hard to find these days."

Torn left the table and went through the door into the storeroom. An oil lamp illuminated a windowless room filled with crates of freighted liquor, boxes of empty bottles, casks of St. Louis beer. There was the back door leading to an alley, barred from the inside. Torn decided against using it, opting instead for the floor hatch. He had to move a stack of casks to get to it, and Frank gave him a hand.

"Give me two minutes to get into place," said Torn,

handing the barkeep his hat and frock coat. "Oh, and there's something in the inside pocket that means a lot to me."

"Don't worry. They'll probably just shoot me in the back and be done with it." A laconic smile played briefly across Frank's dour features.

"If that happens, rest assured they'll be buried alongside you."

"That's strong consolation," Frank joked.

Torn dropped down through the hatch.

CHAPTER

19

THE LADY GAY, LIKE MOST STRUCTURES IN WICHITA, was built on a foundation of beams and pilings. There was a clearance of about two feet. Torn crawled toward Market Street. He had a long way to go—the entire length of the saloon. He couldn't see much, and was glad of it. The earth smelled old and dank, and a lot of trash, some of it sour-smelling, had collected under here. One thing was certain. After this he would definitely have to see about that change of clothes.

He heard footsteps overhead and, a moment later, the open and shut of the front doors, followed by the rap of boot heels on the boardwalk. Torn kept crawling. Then he heard the sound of someone running in the alley between the Lady Gay and the next building to the south. Torn was angling that way, and quickly emerged into the alley. He moved to the front corner of the adjacent building, peered cautiously around. There was Frank, strolling south, several boardwalks away. But Torn didn't see anyone else. He glanced north, across the front of the Lady Gay. Market Street was quiet, dark and empty. Word was already out that there was a good prospect of gun trouble coming to Wichita, and a lot of wise folks were going to stay off the streets as much as possible until the storm had blown over.

Torn glanced behind him, down the alley, then around the corner and south again. This time he spotted the shape of a man emerging from the dark shadows of the next alley down. Torn could see enough to tell that the man was facing away from him and watching Frank. He waited until the man stepped out to follow the Lady Gay barkeep, then stepped out himself, drawing the Colt, and thumbing back the hammer as he drew a bead between the man's shoulder blades.

The man heard the snicker of the Peacemaker's action and froze.

"Grab air and turn around slowly," said Torn.

The man complied, and as Torn stepped closer he saw that it was the Irish conductor who had offered him a seat in the Pullman at Pitchfork Slough.

"Judge Torn!" The railroader wanted to turn his head as Frank doubled back and came up behind him, but the Colt kept his undivided attention.

"What are you doing?" snapped Torn.

"I wanted to talk to you."

"You have a funny way of going about it."

"I-I had to make sure we weren't seen together."

Frank said, "Want I should search him, Mr. Torn?"

Torn listened to his instincts and made a snap judgment. "No. You can go on now. I'll handle it from here. Thanks for your help."

"My pleasure." The barkeep shed the coat, handed it

and the hat to Torn as he passed. "I'll go back and tell Mr. Judah that it worked out."

Torn holstered the Colt. He put his hat and coat back on, and said, "You can put your hands down."

The conductor threw nervous glances up and down the dark street. "Can we get out of the street?" He nodded in the direction of the alley.

"Sure. But if this is a trap, you'll be one step ahead of me at the gates of Hell."

"No trap. I'm on your side, Judge." The Irishman stepped into the alley, and put his back to a wall. He was wearing a shapeless black coat with the collar turned up, and a beret slanted low over his forehead. It troubled Torn to see a brave man so afraid.

"The railroad isn't going to fight Ike Dobson," said the crum boss.

"So I've learned."

"I shouldn't even be talking to you. The word is out that no one with the Santa Fe is to get involved."

"So why are you?"

"I'm not. Not really. It isn't that I don't want to. It tears at my guts that I cannot. I dare not. If I did—well, you remember I told you about the switchman who was crushed between two cars at Emporia? That might happen to me if I stepped forward."

"Are you saying that the railroad..."

"I'm not saying anything. The railroad won't help you, Judge. And I *can't* help you. But I know someone who will. You remember the station agent Pitchfork Slough? Schuyler? His son, Case. The boy saw his own father murdered."

Torn recalled the pale, freckle-faced, sandy-haired youngster walking the rails, showing off for Mary.

"Case was hiding in the slough when Dobson and his men rode up. He saw Dobson talking to his father, and then one of the cowboys shot Mrs. Dobson's horse. After that, the man you threw off the train came up and spoke to Dobson."

"The gambler," said Torn, with distaste. "I should have killed him right off."

"Case says Dobson and his father went into the depot. They came out a few minutes later. They seemed to be arguing. Then Dobson gave a signal, and the man who had shot the horse fired at Schuyler. The poor lad saw his father killed right in front of his eyes." The Irishman shook his head. "It was cold-blooded murder."

"I'm sorry for the boy."

"Aye. So am I. But he'll be well cared for. Every man on the road will be a father to him. I can vouch for that. What bothers me most is Case himself. He hasn't shed a tear that I've seen. He speaks of it all with a kind of . . . a kind of dull calm."

"I don't want to bring him into this," said Torn.

"But he wants to help. He's heard the talk. About how you'll have to stand alone against Dobson. He asked me to come to you. It was the least I could do."

"It's too dangerous. Get him away from here."

The conductor threw a furtive look up the alley. "Aye. That would be best. But he won't want to go. He's got man-sized courage and determination, that boy." He stuck out his hand, searching Torn's face, hoping to find exoneration. "I wish you luck. I wish I could do more. But I . . . it's a terrible thing when you find out that you're not nearly as brave as you've made yourself out to be."

Torn shook the man's hand. "Don't be too hard on yourself. Just take care of Case."

The Irishman took a couple of steps deeper into the alley's gloom, turned back.

"I won't be able to get the lad away until tomorrow,

when the first train rolls through. If you change your mind, come to the yard."

Torn stood in the shadows a moment, brooding, after the conductor had gone. The tragedy of Case Schuyler strengthened his resolve to bring Ike Dobson down. He refused to dwell on the odds that were stacked against him. He could hardly believe that everyone was content to let the matter drop and allow murderers to go free. But there it was. Some people, it seemed, were above the law.

He crossed Market, and worked his way toward the river, using alleys and sidestreets, keeping to the deepest shadow, and seeing no one. A stray growled at him, then skulked away. Torn smiled crookedly. Not even a half-wild dog wanted to have anything to do with him.

Like every other trail town of consequence, Wichita had its crib street, with drab rows of wooden shacks where prostitutes lived and plied their trade. Even the darkness of night failed to hide the ugliness of these stark, miserable quarters. Here on the "line," even at this hour, there were signs of life. A woman sat on a stool in her doorway, smoking a quirly. Another quartered out into the street— not much wider than an alley—to bump into Torn. He thought at first that her clumsiness was a ploy, but when she slurred her words over a salacious suggestion he could tell she was drunk. That, or under the influence of belladonna or morphine. He gave her a close look, then brushed past her, heart pounding. What would he do if Judah's lead panned out, and he found Melony here in this squalor?

One thing at a time, he cautioned himself. He would look for Melony tomorrow. Assuming he was still alive tomorrow.

He stopped at one of the shacks on the north side of the line. The door was shut. Stained and tattered green velvet curtains covered the single window, leaking lamp-light from within. He tapped on the door once, then twice more.

"Who is it?"

"Torn."

She opened the door, the woman he knew only as Babe. The look on her round white face, framed by black hair in ringlets, alarmed him.

"What's wrong? Where's Mary?" he demanded.

She stepped back, and he came after her. The door caught him across the chest, throwing him off-balance. He fell, overturning a small table, and reaching for the gun at his side.

"Don't do it," advised the man who had been concealed behind the door, and who now stood with his back against the wall. There were pistols in both hands—old cap-and-ball Remingtons—and they were aimed rock-steady at Torn.

Torn left his own gun alone.

"Who the hell are you?" he rasped, angry with himself for blundering into ambush.

"Mary's brother. I've come to take her home."

CHAPTER 20

HE WAS TALL AND WIDE-SHOULDERED, HIS BROAD features a burnished copper hue. Deep lines framed a turned-down mouth, and his brown eyes were narrowed and cold. His black hair, square-cut, was shoulder length. He had the look of a hard man who had endured a hard life. Torn figured he was in his twenties, but had the experience of a man twice his age. And Torn could see in his eyes that he had killed before—and would kill now without hesitation.

The Remingtons were early war models, built to the Beal's patent, .44 caliber with eight-inch octagonal barrels. When not pointed at somebody, they rode in cross-draw holsters belted high on the man's lean hips. There was a fleece-lined percussion-cap pouch looped on the belt to the right of the buckle. A larger leather flap pouch, attached to a wide shoulder strap, rested behind the right-side holster. In this pouch, guessed Torn, the man carried his paper cartridges, and maybe a nipple pick and some cleaning patches.

It was the kind of gun that Torn saw less and less of these days, as metal cartridges became less expensive and more commonplace. Sometimes the percussion cap fell off the chamber nipple at the most inopportune time, and these guns generally required more time to load. To alleviate the latter problem, some cap-and-ball men carried spare, already-loaded cylinders.

The man wore buckskin pants tucked into brown spurless jackboots. His shirt was blue flannel, his hat an ordinary Kossuth. A beaded hat band sported the yellow and red sawtooth design popular among the Seminoles.

Torn looked away from the man and the Remingtons. The shack was so small that there was hardly room for the narrow brass bed in one corner, a small dresser with a washbowl and pitcher in another, and a coal-burning stove in a third. A couple of garish dresses hung on nails driven into the walls. The walls were made of shakes, and were quite thin. Most of the shacks on the crib street were so ramshackle that a good wind could knock them down. There was only one door and one window. A lamp on the dresser issued an amber light that softened the stark countenance of the room.

Mary stood over by the dresser and Babe was in the corner by the stove. They both looked apprehensive; the former was afraid that her brother was going to shoot Torn—or more precisely that Torn would do something foolish and *force* her brother to shoot him—and the latter was fearful that Torn would be angry at her for not warning him.

"It's all right, Babe," he said.

"I'm sorry, Clay. I couldn't think what to do. I've been shot once before. God, I can still remember the pain..."

Mary slipped a curious sidelong look at Babe. When she and Torn had arrived, shortly after sunset, Babe had seemed so happy to see Torn that Mary had immediately assumed they were intimate. But Babe, reading Mary better than Mary could read herself, was quick to explain that this was not the case. Not that she would have minded. But Torn had never made any advances, always pretending to miss the hints Babe occasionally made. No, they were just friends; Torn had helped her out of some legal trouble. Now, Mary wondered if there was a connection between that trouble and the time Babe had been shot . . .

Torn turned his attention to Mary. "Is this your brother?"

"Yes. His name is John Chubb."

Without taking his eyes off of him, Chubb asked, "Is this Torn?"

"Yes. This is the man who helped me get away."

The Seminole nodded, but his expression didn't soften, and he didn't lower the Remingtons.

"I'm grateful for that, Mr. Torn. I hope I won't have to kill you. That would make me feel bad."

"Me, too," said Torn.

"She tells me you want her to testify against Dobson. She won't. She is coming home with me. The council has sent me to bring her, and I must not fail. Our own grandfather, Billy Bowlegs, chief of the Northern Seminole, has my promise that I will deliver Mary safely to his side. She cannot help you. It is not safe. And I do not like that she must hide in this place."

Babe snorted. "What? My place ain't good enough for your sister, is that it?"

"Babe."

"Aw, hell, Clay. I'm sorry again. It's just that this big sonuvabitch scared me." Embarrassed, Babe glanced sheepishly at Mary. "And my apologies to you for my language."

"No, it is I who should apologize."

Chubb said, "Now that the apologies are out of the way, we'd better be going, Mary."

"Mind if I stand up?" asked Torn.

"You do what you want."

Torn didn't miss the hidden meaning in that statement. It didn't matter that much to John Chubb whether he stayed on the floor or got to his feet—and neither did it matter to the Seminole if he went for his gun and died, or didn't and stayed alive. Torn got up, slowly, and kept his right hand well away from his body.

"Ike Dobson must be stopped," he said. "He and his men are killing innocent people. I need your sister's help to stop him."

"No," said Chubb bluntly. "She should never have left her people. Whites have always been trouble for the Seminole. Mary should not have forgotten this. Any time we let the white man into our lives, our lives are ruined."

Mary, downcast, silently accepted this reprimand.

"Mary has the right to decide for herself," argued Torn.

"No. She left against the wishes of her family and the council. Now she has asked for our help, and she must abide by our decision."

Torn stared at Mary, feeling betrayed. "You sent for him?"

"Yes."

Chubb said, "I have been in this town almost a week. Like everyone else, I heard of the fight on the train. I wanted to go out and search for you and Mary, but I knew that this would be a waste of time. So I waited for you to come here. Where else could you go, with Dobson after you? While I waited, I asked around. Found out you had two friends here, Torn. A saloon owner and a whore. I figured you would go to one or the other for help."

Torn was still staring at Mary.

"A couple of weeks ago a peddler passed through the Bar ID," she explained. "He was on his way to the Nations from St. Louis, where he had bought trade goods. He agreed to take a message to my tribe. He was, I think, more interested in improving his standing with my people than he was afraid of my husband. I asked that someone meet me in Wichita. I wasn't sure when I would escape, but I knew that it would have to be soon. I couldn't stand it any longer. That's why I rode for the train to Wichita. Why I was at Pitchfork Slough in the first place."

"Have you forgotten the woman and child?" asked Torn quietly. "The vow you made, to see that Dobson answered for his crimes?"

"I haven't forgotten," she snapped back, distraught. "But I must obey my brother and the council."

Sensing Torn's bitter disappointment, Chubb said, "Don't blame her. She doesn't have a choice. If you must blame anyone, blame your own people. Why should a Seminole be concerned with the white man's problems? What has the white man done, that he should expect the Seminole people to get involved in his fights? We made the mistake of doing that once before, in the big war. What did we get in return? Grief and broken promises." Chubb shook his head. "No. This is not our fight. You have no right to expect my sister's help."

"You're right," said Torn. "Her well-being is more important. Go with your brother, Mary. Go while you still can. They're coming. I haven't seen them or heard them. But I know. There's no time to waste."

CHAPTER 21

MARY STARED AT TORN WITH A STRICKEN EXPRES-
sion on her face. She didn't understand how it could have
happened in so short a time, but the prospect of leaving
this man weighed heavily on her heart. She fought back a
flood of tears.

Torn started to turn away from Chubb and the door. As
he did, he saw that the Seminole was lowering the brace
of Remingtons just a fraction. Chubb was dropping his
guard; he wasn't even consciously aware, yet, that he had
bought the bill of goods Torn had been trying to sell.

Because Torn had no intention of letting them just walk
out.

It wasn't that he wanted Mary to stay against her will.
If she freely chose to go home, then fine, he would fight
Ike Dobson alone, and harbor no ill will toward her. But
apparently she wasn't free to choose her own course.
Apparently, the help of her brother and the tribal council

had strings attached. She had forsaken her tribe, and now that she wanted back into the fold, she had to abide by their terms. Torn knew that the only way he would get an honest answer out of Mary was by taking John Chubb out.

And he wasn't partial to being bushwhacked and then held at gunpoint, no matter who it was.

As he turned, he swept the room again, this time looking for the Winchester. He had left the repeater behind. Not that Mary and Babe needed any more hardware, necessarily. Like most girls on the line, Babe would have a couple of pistols and at least one dagger among her possessions. And Mary still had the hogleg he had taken from the Bar ID cowboy during the fight on the train. He assumed that she still had the gambler's hideout derringer, too, though he had lost track of it during their flight across the prairie. That hideout still had one loaded barrel.

Not that he expected her to use the guns to his benefit, against her own brother. Babe might, if the opportunity presented itself. But he didn't want Chubb shot—just disarmed. He didn't want to kill John Chubb. Unfortunately, the Seminole was not restrained by a similar consideration.

All this flashed through his mind in seconds, as he was turning, and he seemed to trip over the table he had overturned a moment before, losing his balance. It was a small, round pedestal table of cherrywood, once a handsome piece of furniture that had seen hard times. Stumbling, Torn reached down to catch himself, grasping the table at the base with his left hand. Spinning, he threw it with all his might at John Chubb. He was hoping that one thing would work in his favor: that Chubb might hesitate if it came down to firing those big Remingtons in such small confines, for fear of accidentally harming Mary.

As soon as he hurled the table, Torn lunged at Chubb.

The Seminole tried to bat the table away with his arms, and before he could bring the Remingtons to bear once more, Torn hit him hard, slamming him against the wall with an impact that made the entire flimsy structure shudder. Torn drove his right fist up under Chubb's chin, and saw the Seminole's eyes glaze momentarily. But Chubb was one tough customer. As Torn got his hand on the barrel of the Remington in Chubb's left hand and twisted savagely, wrenching the pistol free, Chubb struck Torn across the side of the head with the gun in his right hand.

Blinded by a dazzling display of swirling lights, Torn felt his legs go rubbery, and he pitched to the floor. He managed to keep a grip on the Remington from Chubb's left hand, and Chubb let him take it down with him as he fell. The Seminole aimed the other gun at Torn. Mary screamed something. Torn couldn't quite make it out through the roar in his ears, a sound like that made by a raging river. He lashed out with a kick that, miraculously, connected, sending the Remington spinning out of Chubb's grasp. Still groggy from the blow to the head, Torn forced himself to his feet. Everything tilted nauseatingly one way and then the other. He was reminded of a trip once taken on a keelboat through the rapids of the White River.

Then Chubb hit him like a boulder rolling down a mountain. Their legs got tangled up, and Torn found himself falling again. He pulled his knees up and then straightened his legs when he hit the floor. Chubb went somersaulting over him and right out through the doorway. Rolling over, Torn gathered himself up and charged. Chubb got up and curtailed the charge with a left hook that dropped Torn to the planks of the sidewalk outside the front of the shack. Torn hooked an arm behind Chubb's knee and yanked the Seminole off his feet.

Torn again picked himself up, in time to see John Chubb

reach a hand behind his back as he, too, rose. When Torn saw that hand again it held an Arkansas Toothpick, twelve inches of straight, sharply pointed, double-edged steel death. Dropping into the knife-fighter's crouching stance, Chubb moved sideways into the dark street.

Torn thought briefly of the Colt Peacemaker on his hip, then decided against it. Chubb was probably a better man with a blade than he was, but that was no excuse for using a gun on someone armed with a blade. Torn had always known that one day his sense of fair play would be the end of him. Quite probably, this was the day.

He reached under his coat, thumbed the rawhide thong from the pommel of the saber-knife, and felt the weapon drop into his waiting hand.

Knife-fighting was an art. Torn had seen some real masters firsthand, and he was a quick learner. Dropping into the crouch, he kept his feet wide apart and his body and head well back, the saber-knife extended in his right hand, the blade parallel with the ground. They circled each other in the street. Torn heard Mary cry out for them to stop, but he didn't take his eyes off Chubb, so he didn't see Mary try to throw herself between them, or Babe as she physically restrained the other woman.

Chubb darted in, making a sweeping thrust at Torn's belly. Torn jumped backwards, caught the passing blade with his own and tried to throw his adversary off balance by pushing it sharply to the side. Chubb was quick and sure-footed. He lashed out with a backhand, upwards swipe that had Torn retreating again, the point of the Arkansas Toothpick missing his face by a prayer. Blade rang against blade as Chubb thrust again. Torn parried with the saber-knife, carrying the Arkansas Toothpick past him, and stepped in to punch Chubb in the face. The Seminole staggered backward on his heels. Torn closed in, but in his eagerness to seize the advantage, almost walked into a gut-ripping sweep. He caught Chubb's blade with his own, driving the stroke outward and away from himself. The point of the Arkansas Toothpick rent his frock coat. He slashed at Chubb and the Seminole ducked. Torn kicked him in the face. Chubb reeled away, blood spewing from his mouth as he sprawled in the dust.

Torn moved in with more caution this time, going over in his mind the basic rules of knife combat. Rip upward, thrust downward. The best target was the torso, more specifically downward from the breastbone. But Torn was still reluctant to go for the killing blow. If he could cut open Chubb's knife arm, then the fight would probably be over.

Chubb bounced back up into a crouch, border-shifting his knife from hand to hand, showing new respect for Torn's fighting abilities.

Torn was all set to move in when he heard the drumming thunder of hooves. A great many horses at the gallop. A woman screamed—not Mary this time, but someone further up the street. The knife fight had brought some spectators out of the cribs. Mostly prostitutes, in various stages of undress, with a few male customers in a similar condition. Now these folks were scurrying for cover as riders came pounding up and down the street from both directions. Before Torn could think what to do they were on him, forming two tight ranks on their snorting, prancing mounts, not twenty feet apart, with him in the middle. Some of them held torches, pine pitch on stout lengths of wood.

A quick scan didn't reveal any faces that he recognized, but he knew full well who they were. And though they had never met before, he knew which man was Ike Dobson. Mary had started to flee back into Babe's shack, but the big man's booming voice froze her in her tracks.

"You run any more, woman, I'll just kill you and be done with it."

Babe stepped close to Mary, put a comforting arm around her shoulders and glared defiantly at Dobson.

But Dobson paid no attention to the soiled dove. His sun-faded eyes swung from Torn to Chubb—the Seminole struggling to his feet, his face bloodied—and finally back to Torn.

"You must be the one that killed my men and run off with my wife. I got a little something for you."

And Ike Dobson reached for his gun.

CHAPTER

22

IN THAT SINGLE SECOND, AS DOBSON'S HAND
dropped to the gun on his hip, Torn experienced an odd
exhilaration. It occurred to him that this was the best way
for it to happen. A quick and certain way to see justice
done—justice from a gunbarrel rather than from between
the leatherbound covers of a statute book. There was
nothing wrong with that kind of justice. Of course, he would
die serving it up. But that was a small price to pay. His
only regret would be Melony—he'd never know what had
become of Melony . . .

He tossed the saber-knife from right hand to left, and
his right streaked to the Colt Peacemaker, and he drew
the revolver—all this in less time than it took Dobson to
get his hand on his own gun. They weren't the only ones
slapping leather—everybody was going for his iron. Except Chubb, of course, whose Remingtons were on the
floor in Babe's shack. But Torn figured he was a shade

quicker than any of the Bar ID cowboys, and all he needed was one shot.

The shotgun blast came from behind him; he flinched involuntarily, and still managed to carry the draw through, shifting his body sideways. It was something a man learned in war. Fire on the move, and you don't give the enemy a stationary target. Some men couldn't hit an elephant at point-blank range without planting their feet, but Torn had discovered that movement did not impair his shooting one whit.

Everybody jumped when the scattergun spoke. So did the horses. Dobson jerked rein without meaning to. His mount reared up just as Torn fired. The bullet smashed through the animal's jaw and slanted up into the brain. The horse dropped in its tracks.

Mass confusion reigned. Horses pivoted, men shouted, guns went off. A slug plucked at Torn's frock coat, but left him unscathed. He saw Chubb throw the Arkansas Toothpick. It was a fighting knife, poorly balanced for throwing, but Chubb didn't let that stop him. Torn didn't wait to see if the Seminole hit his mark. He was running, emptying the Peacemaker without taking careful aim. The riders were so tightly packed in the street that he figured he was bound to hit something.

A bullet burned like fire as it grazed his side. Another struck the heel of his boot, kicking his leg out from under him. He fell, rolled over onto his back and looked up at a rearing horse coming down on top of him. He kept rolling. The rider tried to get a shot at him from astride the snorting, wild-eyed horse, and missed cleanly. Torn swept the Colt into line and pulled the trigger. The hammer fell on an empty chamber. He swore as the Bar ID man got set to fire again. He never got the shot off. John Chubb came flying through the air and carried the cowboy out of the saddle. They struck the sidewalk hard enough to splinter planking. Chubb got up. The cowboy didn't; he had taken the brunt of the fall. Chubb dived through the doorway into Babe's crib. Torn went through the window, not caring to wait until Chubb cleared the doorway.

He fell in a shower of glass and splintered frame, kicked out of a tangle of green velvet drapery, powered to his feet, and collided with Babe, knocking her on her duff. He lunged for the Winchester. The sound of bullets smacking into wood was loud in his ears as he dropped the empty Colt into its holster. "Mary! Get down!" he yelled, although he wasn't sure exactly where Mary was. Grabbing the repeater, he smashed the lamp chimney with the saber-knife, extinguishing the flame and plunging the room into darkness. Only partial darkness; orange torchlight leaked through the doorway and the shattered window, making shadows dance.

"Don't shoot, you bastards!" It was Dobson's bullhorn voice, atremble with rage. "Mary's in there, goddammit!"

The shooting stopped.

"Mary," breathed Torn.

"I'm all right." The reassurance came from the floor to his right. He saw her huddled half-under the brass bed. Chubb was crawling toward her.

"Woman!" bellowed Dobson. "You got one minute to get out here or..."

Another shotgun blast shattered the momentary lull. A barrage of sidegun and rifle fire answered, but this wasn't directed at the shack. Torn couldn't quite figure it out, but he didn't waste a lot of time pondering. That they were trapped was the thought foremost in his mind. There was no exit except out under the Bar ID guns. So he had to *make* an exit.

Clutching the repeater with both hands, he drove the

stock as hard as he could against the rear wall. The brass
butt-plate splintered a shake. He struck again and again
and again. These cribs were poorly constructed, the walls
so thin that they couldn't keep the winter out. Torn kept
hammering away, felt himself breaking out into a cold
sweat. He had a strong aversion to being closed up somewhere against his will.

"Thanks, Clay," said Babe, laconic, resting where the
collision with Torn had put her. "I always wanted a back
door."

Torn kicked away a few shattered lengths of wood, and
perceived that the ragged hole he had made was large
enough for a man to worm through.

"Chubb, get your sister out."

Two men came charging through the doorway. Torn
whirled and swung the Winchester. The barrel caught one
man across the head. Babe cursed like a sergeant as the
body fell on top of her. The other Bar ID man slammed
into Torn, driving him backward. They smashed into the
dresser, rendering it into so much kindling, shattering the
porcelain washbowl and pitcher. They fell into a pile of
broken wood and silky unmentionables. Torn felt the man
convulse and then go limp. He rolled the body off of him
and pulled the saber-knife out of the dead man's chest,
feeling the blade grate against bone and the wash of hot
blood on his hand.

"Babe," he said looking gravely down at the dead man,
"get out."

She crawled out through the hole, tearing her lace-
hemmed cotton wrapper on a jagged edge. Wiping the
blade clean on his trouser leg, Torn sheathed the saber-
knife, then followed her, emerging into a narrow, trash-
filled alley. Babe was swearing enthusiastically, trying to
hold the garment together in what was, Torn thought, a

curious display of modesty, considering the woman's line of work.

He saw no sign of Chubb and Mary. He was sure they had gotten out of the shack. He grabbed Babe's hand and started to run. No time to worry about Mary and her brother now. It wouldn't take Dobson long to discover that they had slipped out of his grasp.

In fact, it didn't take any time at all. He heard the sound of galloping horses, a man shout "There they go!" and the boom of revolvers. A bullet sang past, too close. Torn shoved Babe roughly to the ground. She sprawled, pale legs uncovered and gleaming like milkglass in the darkness. Spinning, Torn dropped to one knee and brought the Winchester to his shoulder. A pair of riders thundered down the alley toward them. He saw the muzzle flash of their guns. Despite what Mary had said about them, these Bar ID bravos, it seemed, were more cowpunchers than shootists. How many of them, he wondered, were going to have to die on account of Ike Dobson's injured pride? Then he ceased to contemplate imponderables, for as he tried to lever a shell into the rifle's breech, the repeater jammed.

He wasn't surprised. Rifles were not designed for the battering down of walls and the clubbing of men. But it left him in a bad spot because his Peacemaker was empty and the charging horsemen were a heartbeat away from being right on top of him.

"Babe!" he yelled. "Run!"

A shotgun boomed. One of the riders somersaulted over the back of his horse. Torn rose up, with the Winchester held like a club, ran forward and swung with all his might, aiming for the forelegs of the second man's horse. The impact jerked the smashed repeater out of his grasp. The animal shrieked and toppled forward, throwing its rider thirty feet. Torn was struck by the falling horse and thrown violently sideways.

He got up slowly. The rider lay still. The horse was on its side, thrashing in a futile attempt to rise. Torn grimly fed a couple of shells into the Colt, stepped up and, seeing that one of the forelegs was fractured, put a bullet through the animal's head.

The sound of footfalls spun him around.

Wyatt Earp emerged from the obscuring gloom of the alley, a 12-gauge Greener shouldered-racked. He looked as casual and carefree as a man enjoying an evening constitutional.

"I should have known," said Torn.

Wyatt glanced at the dead horse. "That was property of the United States Cavalry, wasn't it, Clay? Still fighting the war?"

"Not that one. Another. Don't start on me, Wyatt."

Wyatt smiled lazily. He looked remarkably relaxed, considering the circumstances. A ragged volley of gunfire rang out from the crib street.

"Wonder what they're shooting at, with us over here?" mused Earp.

"Probably innocent bystanders," replied Torn dryly.

Babe was picking herself up. Wyatt gave her a hand. She glowered at him.

"About damn time. What the hell do we each pay you a dollar a month for, anyway?"

"What was that?" queried Torn sharply.

Wyatt looked like a boy caught with his hand in the cookie jar. "Oh, it's just a little agreement I have with the girls on the line."

"It's a racket called protection," clarified Babe.

Torn smiled grimly. Indeed, he *should* have known that

Wyatt Earp's motive for dealing himself in was profit rather than principle.

"Come on," urged Wyatt. "Let's make dust."

They left the alley, cut between two buildings and crossed the street that ran parallel to the line and north of it. They paused in the shadows that gathered thickly between a drugstore and a barber shop, checked their backtrail. There was no evidence of pursuit. Taking this opportunity to reload the Peacemaker, Torn could scarcely believe that he had gotten out of that one alive. He wondered about Mary and her brother.

"Oh sweet Jesus," whispered Babe.

He looked sharply at her, then followed her stricken gaze toward the crib street, saw the orange glow pushing back the night, the drift of smoke, the tongue of flame leaping above the rooftops.

"Damn," he said.

"Why would he do that?" wondered Wyatt, no longer cool and casual.

"Spite," said Torn. "He's full of it."

"The bastard," said Babe, fervently.

They heard the drumming of horses at the gallop. Torn listened with bated breath, but instead of getting louder, the sound quickly faded.

Dobson and his Bar ID boys were calling it a night.

23

NEXT MORNING, TORN WAS FINISHING HIS BREAK-
fast when Judge Stephens, accompanied by Wyatt Earp,
entered the Douglas Street hash house. Stephens was
more florid than usual. A rolled-up newspaper was clutched
like a club in one white-knuckled fist. The pair approached
Torn's corner table. There were a dozen other patrons in
the restaurant and they all stopped eating to watch warily,
expecting trouble.

Stephens threw the paper on the table and tried to loom
over Torn—a difficult task for one so short and round.
Torn could see that the paper was the special edition of
the Wichita *Eagle*, hot off the Washington two-pull press
this very morning.

"Have you read this?" snapped Stephens.

Torn, sipping coffee, nodded briefly.

Stephens snatched the paper up, opened it with a violent
jerk of the arms, and read: " 'Notice: to one Ike Dobson

and his gang of thugs and cutthroats. The citizens of Wichita cordially invite you one and all to return at your earliest convenience to this fair city, at which time a grand necktie party will be put on for your benefit, with you as the guests of honor, the expense of which will be borne with pleasure by the community as a whole.'"

"Has a nice ring to it."

Stephens dropped the paper on the table with epic disgust. "It goes on, in lurid detail, to recount the unsubstantiated accusations of a boy who claims Ike Dobson had his father, the Pitchfork Slough station agent, murdered. I have the feeling you are behind that."

"Unsubstantiated?" echoed Torn, coldly. "The *corpus delicti* was buried yesterday."

Losing Mary had caused him to rethink the idea of using Case Schuyler against Dobson. He had taken the boy to the newspaper, and then seen him safely aboard the morning westbound.

Stephens squeezed the bridge of his nose with thumb and forefinger.

"My congratulations, sir. You have managed to swing public opinion against Ike Dobson."

"I didn't do that. Dobson did it all by himself. He might have burned Wichita to the ground. Luckily, the wind drove the fire his men started into the river."

"It's a fine thing: a federal judge inciting the population to vigilante action."

"Now that," said Torn, "is an unsubstantiated accusation."

"I've been hounded all morning long," complained Stephens, miserably. "And I have concluded that we must issue warrants for Ike Dobson and his men." Stephens turned to Earp. "Where in tarnation is Marshal Meagher?"

"Out of town," replied Wyatt wryly. "On personal business."

Stephens grunted. "Then it falls to you, deputy, to prepare to place Ike Dobson, along with any and all of his employees, under arrest, should they set foot across the city limits. I authorize you to deputize as many citizens as you need. I doubt that you will want for volunteers."

"Fat lot of good that will do," said Torn. "Mary Dobson is on her way to the Indian Nations."

"What? How do you know?"

"I know. And sooner or later, Dobson will find out."

"The Indian Nations," murmured Wyatt. "That's out of my jurisdiction. What a shame."

"I can tell you're real disappointed, Wyatt," said Torn.

"Then I must request help from the U.S. Marshals," sighed Stephens. "I'll wire Topeka immediately." With one final unfriendly glower at Torn, he left the dining room.

Wyatt Earp didn't wait for an invitation to sprawl in the chair across from Torn. "You look a lot better than when I saw you last."

Torn just nodded. He had finally retrieved his belongings from the depot baggage room, changed into his spare shirt and trousers. A bath and a shave and a brand new black frock coat from Benteen's Haberdashery had done the rest. A doctor had seen to the bullet graze. Now all he needed was sleep. Unfortunately, that was going to have to wait.

"That your rig on the black mare tied up outside?" asked Wyatt.

"You know it is."

"You're going after her, then."

"That's right."

"Isn't that cayuse the property of the cavalry?"

"Call it a requisition."

"What if she doesn't want to come back?"

"That's her choice. But I want to hear it from her."

"Truth is, you know Dobson will go after her, too, and you want to be there for the final reckoning." Wyatt glanced out the window at a street bustling with morning activity. "You sure put Judge Stephens between a rock and a hard place."

"Like I said, Dobson did it himself. He doesn't know when to stop."

"Well, it's one thing to issue a warrant, another to convict him in a court of law."

"You'll never get Ike Dobson into a court of law."

"I wonder how he found out about you and Mrs. Dobson being at Babe's?" murmured Wyatt, staring intently through the window.

Torn followed his gaze. In the shade of the boardwalk across the street he saw Stephens in animated conversation with the tinhorn gambler in the gray claw hammer coat and white Panama.

He looked at Wyatt. Earp looked at him. They were entertaining the same notion.

"What's his handle?" asked Torn.

"Fontane. Dice Fontane."

The last card hasn't been dealt yet. No one messes with Dice Fontane . . .

Torn said, "I remember now. He told me himself. I just didn't think it was very important at the time. And to think that I once had my knife at his throat."

"Never put off until tomorrow what's better done today," said Wyatt. "That's my motto."

Torn stood up to leave, putting four bits on the table, then handing Wyatt two big gold double eagles.

"What's this for?" asked Earp, startled.

"Babe. Give it to her for me, will you? All of it."

Wyatt pretended that the last comment injured his feelings. "Now just what kind of a man do you think I am, Clay?"

"I don't know, Wyatt," admitted Torn. "I guess only time will tell." Turning away, he had a thought, and took the daguerreotype from the inside breast pocket of his new coat, holding it out in front of Wyatt. "You know all the girls on the line. Have you seen her?"

Pursing his lips, Wyatt gave the photograph a careful study. Torn felt his heart pounding in his chest.

Wyatt shook his head. "There's a girl who looks some like her. Calls herself Lillie Smith. But that's not her. Why?"

Torn pocketed the daguerreotype, experiencing an unaccountable mixture of disappointment and relief.

"It's not important," he replied, walking away.

CHAPTER 24

DICE FONTANE FOUND IKE DOBSON AND THE BAR ID
bunch five miles west of Wichita, in the precious shade of
a few scrawny cottonwoods lining the banks of a shallow
creek.

The gambler slowed the broomtail he had rented from
a Wichita livery to a bone-jarring trot and rode slow and
easy into camp. After seeing their handiwork at Pitchfork
Slough, he was afraid of them. He tried not to let it show,
nodding at the stern and silent men, a friendly smile pasted
on his face.

The Bar ID men weren't smiling. They looked haggard
and hostile. Their faces were masked with pale, sweat-
streaked dust. Their eyes were dulled from exhaustion.
Almost all of them were lying down. It looked as though
they had barely managed to dismount and unsaddle before
collapsing right on the spot. A few of them were working
on corn dodgers and beef jerky. A couple of others were

lethargically cleaning their weapons. More than a few were staring off into the distance, too weary to even sleep.

Someone had built a fire out of "prairie coal," and one man was nursing a pot of coffee. Fontane had been in the West long enough to know that buffalo and cow chips burned slow and hot and even, but he still wasn't completely comfortable with the concept. As he rode by, the man lifted the hinged top of the pot, saw that the muddy-brown brew was boiling, and poured a cup of cold water in to settle the grounds.

The cardsharp saw Ike Dobson standing, hands on hips, over where the horses had been picketed. A couple of lass-ropes had been tied together and the line was strung between two trees. The mounts tethered to this stake rope looked every bit as played out as the men. Fontane angled the rented horse that way.

As he neared, Fontane noticed that two men were laid out on their blankets and a third was sitting on his, shirtless, with his back resting against the rough trunk of a cottonwood. One of the prone men had a head wound. It was bandaged with what appeared to be strips of material torn from a flannel shirt. The other man's leg wore a splint fashioned from a rifle and more strips of flannel.

Fontane checked his mount. Ike Dobson gave him the merest glance, then turned his attention back to the activities of a cowboy who was tending to the shirtless man. No one said a word. The only sounds the gambler heard were the wind in the trees, the chuckling of the creek, the hiss of the boiling coffee, and the whicker of a horse.

The cowboy who squatted in front of the shirtless man fished a block of phosphorous matches out of a vest pocket and snapped one off.

"This'll burn some," he said.

The shirtless man forced a smile. "Ned, I reckon it will. It's gunpowder, ain't it?"

Ned flicked the match to life with a thumbnail and stood up. At that moment Fontane saw the bleeding hole high up on the other man's chest, just below the collarbone. It was plastered with gunpowder. Ned bent and touched the burning strike-anywhere to it. The gunpowder flared in a puff of smoke. The wounded cowboy's lips pulled back in a snarling rictus of pain, his body heaving in a rigid convulsion. But he didn't make a sound. Fontane felt suddenly queasy. These men awed him. They were hard, stoic men. The gambler knew, with humbling certainty, that he could not have endured a gunpowder cauterization without screaming or fainting, or both in quick succession. But when it was done, the shirtless cowboy tucked his chin to look at the powder-burned patch of skin and force another smile.

"That did smart some, Ned, but I ain't bleedin' like a stuck pig no more."

Ned turned to Ike Dobson with a curt nod. "He'll do. Tanner's got plenty of fur on his brisket."

Lute Dobson was standing beside his father. Now he stepped forward and flicked the Arkansas Toothpick that had been snugged under his shellbelt into the ground alongside the man called Tanner.

"There's your keepsake, partner. Maybe you'll get a chance to return it to its rightful owner. Blade first."

Ike now turned and came over to Fontane. The card-sharp remembered, just in time, that it was a serious breach of range etiquette to stay mounted when you spoke to a man afoot, and he swung down quickly, fearing that Dobson might drag him out of the saddle if he did not.

"What do you want?" asked Ike, irascible.

"I have some news you might be interested in, Mr. Dobson."

"I'm listening."

"Your wife is making for the Nations. And Torn rode out this morning, heading south. Odds are he's going after her."

Dobson's jaw worked as pure hatred rippled across his craggy face.

Lute came up, flashing his counterfeit smile at Fontane.

"Judge Stephens tell you to come find us?"

"Nobody tells me to do anything," replied Fontane, striving to sound tougher than he felt in the presence of these dangerous men. "I offered to do it."

"Yeah? Now, why is that? You figure maybe there's some money in it for you?"

Ike looked at his son, but said nothing. Lute sounded like the last thing he wanted to do was pay Fontane for the information.

"I don't want your money," said Fontane resentfully. "I just think it's wrong when a man runs off with another's wife."

He looked from Ike to Lute to Ned, who stood back some from the others, but was still within earshot. As a gambler, Fontane had learned to see behind men's eyes, and he could tell now that, of the three of them, only Ike believed that the real reason Mary Dobson had run away was to be with Clay Torn. And none of them believed that Fontane was genuinely concerned about the sanctity of marriage.

"Truth is," jeered Lute, "you got yourself a grudge against this Torn feller. You want to see him dead. You just hope we'll do the deed for you."

"That's not true," denied Fontane. "And if it ever had been the case, I would no longer hold out much hope that you could, as you say, do the deed. You've had a couple of chances. I gave you the last chance myself. When you rode into Wichita, I was the one who told you where you could find him—and Mrs. Dobson." He looked at Ike. "It wasn't easy, you know. I had to follow Torn without him knowing. If he'd found me out, he would have tried to kill me. But I did it because I thought it only fair that you had first crack at him, Mr. Dobson. In a sense, you have a prior claim."

Ike Dobson drew a long breath. "We'll head for the Nations."

Ned stepped up so quickly that Fontane's horse shied, almost jerking rein leather out of the cardsharp's hand.

"We can't do it, Mr. Dobson."

"Don't rile me, Ned."

But Ned refused to back down. "Look at the men, Mr. Dobson. They're bottomed out. So are the horses. If they don't get rest and grain, we'll be walking before too much longer."

"Then by God, we'll walk. We'll crawl, if we have to."

"Ease off, Ned," warned Lute.

But Ned was too provoked to heed the warning.

"We've lost six men dead. Six more stove up. And Drew. Your son is lying over there somewhere, and he ain't been right since he fell off that train."

"He's a Dobson," grated Ike. "He'll do what has to be done."

"What about the ranch?" Ned persisted. "We're all riding around on this grand tour of Kansas, and the Bar ID's going to hell in a handbasket."

"Damn you, Ned," hissed Dobson, incensed. "If you don't like the lay of the land, move on."

"I've been with you for a lot of years, Mr. Dobson. I've always done what you told me to. But, of late, you've stepped clean over the line. We've all done things that we felt weren't right, but we did them out of loyalty to you. But I guess loyalty will take me just so far."

"You're fired."

Ned nodded bleakly. "I figured that would come of this. But I had to speak my piece. And while I'm at it, I'll say one more thing."

"Don't push your luck," warned Dobson.

Ned didn't seem to hear him. "Long as I've known you, you were a man who saw things the way they were. So it pains me to see you fooling yourself like this. Mrs. Dobson is a fine and decent woman. She never done wrong by you. I reckon she lit out because she couldn't abide seeing what you were doing to yourself, not to mention those sodbusters. This cardsharp's dealing off the bottom. She ain't the kind to run off with another man, and we all know it. Including you, deep down. You just can't let go or admit that you're wrong."

"Are you finished?"

Ned pushed his lips out and in, out and in, then nodded. "That's all I've got to say except so long."

He turned away. They watched him gather up his saddle and blanket and start for the horses. Then Fontane saw Ike Dobson's hand move to the butt of his sidegun. Lute saw this, too, and jumped out of the way, shouting Ned's name. Ned spun, dropping the gear, but he didn't have a prayer. Dobson's revolver boomed. The bullet struck Ned squarely in the chest, lifting him off his feet. He was dead before he hit the ground.

Leery of more gunplay, Fontane looked around to see the other Bar ID riders leaping to their feet. Ike Dobson didn't seem to notice. He was glowering at his son.

"You didn't want to shoot him in the back, did you, Pa?"

Holstering the gun, Dobson turned away from Lute, a

motion sharpened with disgust. Fontane snuck a glance at Lute. Again, he read behind the eyes. And he knew, with conviction based on a gambler's finely-honed instincts, that Lute Dobson had thrown that warning at Ned for a different reason.

He had hoped for an entirely different outcome.

Dobson confronted the rest of the men, his big fists clenched.

"Anybody else wants to pull out, do it now. But keep your traps shut when you do. I won't take back talk, and I won't be called a liar."

The men exchanged grim glances, but no one spoke— and no one made a move to break camp.

Apparently satisfied with this reaction, Dobson spun to face Fontane, who willed himself to stand fast.

"I've got a job for you. Or are you all through helping?"

"I am at your service, sir."

"Go back to Wichita. Put out the word that I need men who don't mind a little gunwork. I reckon, you being what you are, you know men like that."

"Yes, I know men like that," replied Fontane coolly, deeming it wise to ignore the remark that he took to be an aspersion upon his character.

"How many you reckon you can get together?"

"How many do you need?"

Dobson looked around him. "As many as I can get."

"Men like that don't work for nothing."

"They'll be well paid. Any man who won't take Ike Dobson's word for that, I don't want him riding with me."

"That's not it, Mr. Dobson. How do I convince them that I speak for you?"

"He's right, Pa," said Lute. "I'll go with him."

"No," said Fontane hastily. "That would only cause problems. Lot of folks in town are out of sorts with you, after what happened last night." The gambler discreetly decided not to mention the arrest warrant, or the newspaper invitation to a hanging. No point in adding fuel to Dobson's fire.

Dobson snorted. "Like I give a good goddamn about them."

"I'll find the men you need," Fontane assured him. "Then what?"

"Bring 'em where the Arkansas meets the Salt Fork. I'll be there. But I won't wait long. Say, three days from today. We'll pick up fresh mounts on the way."

"What about Tanner and the others?" asked Lute, thumbing over his shoulder at the three injured men suffering in the speckled shade of the cottonwoods.

"What about 'em?" snapped Dobson crossly. "They stay here. We'll leave them with enough grub, and there's plenty of water. They'll make out."

"Maybe somebody ought to stay with them."

Dobson squinted at his son, perplexed. "Since when did you start worrying about others?"

Lute shrugged. "Just seems wrong to leave them to fend for themselves."

"I can't spare a man to wet-nurse them," said Dobson, in a gruff tone that clearly conveyed that this was his final word on the subject.

Fontane wasn't as puzzled as Dobson by Lute's uncharacteristic concern for the wounded. The Bar ID men were close enough to hear the exchange between father and son—which was exactly what Lute had intended. Lute Dobson was one smart scheming son of a bitch, the gambler decided with grudging admiration. One day soon he was going to take a shot at claiming his birthright before it came due, and he wanted to make sure the Bar ID cowboys were loyal to the right Dobson—him. There was no better time to work on that than right now. Ike's obsession with the recovery of his runaway wife had turned many people against him, including one of his own men. It might, in time, do likewise for the rest.

"So what are you lollygaggin' around for?" Dobson barked.

Fontane refused to rile or ruffle. He smiled at Ike with something akin to pity. Like a rabid dog, Dobson was snapping at everyone now. The gambler turned and mounted up. Before he could rein the horse around and kick it into reluctant motion, though, Dobson stepped up to grab hold of the bridle.

"One more thing. I'll pay a thousand dollars to the man who kills Clay Torn. You let that be known. It might make 'em sit up and take notice."

"That might cost you more than money. He is, after all, a federal judge."

"The devil take the cost."

Fontane's coyote eyes flicked to Lute Dobson. "I'm sure he will. Why, I might even have a shot at that bounty myself."

Dobson's smile was wolfish. "I thought you might."

He let go of the bridle. Fontane wheeled the horse around and rode away from camp.

CHAPTER

25

ON THE FOURTH DAY OUT OF WICHITA, CLAY TORN crossed the North Fork of the Canadian and entered the Seminole Nation.

"Sure, a man and a woman crossed yesterday," answered the man who owned and operated the ferry at Groame's Crossing. He and his son were walking the couple cable from bow to stern, muscling the ferry across the wide river. They were halfway to the south bank when Torn asked the question. The current had caught the ferry and was pushing it downstream, bowing the cable into a taut curve. The craft looked sturdy enough, and the cable was two inches thick, as sound as the hawser of a sailing ship, and secured to stout pilings on either bank. Torn held on to the black mare, the reins gathered in one hand up close to the bit rings, the other stroking the horse's muzzle. The mare was not too enthusiastic about the boat ride.

The ferryman's information was some comfort to Torn. He had been pretty sure that Chubb and Mary had escaped Dobson and his men during that violent night in Wichita, but this was the first solid evidence. At least Mary was safe.

"You after them two?" asked the ferryman as he passed Torn.

"Not after them, really," replied Torn, and waited until the burly man passed on his way to the bow and another handful of cable to add, "I hope to meet them in Mikasuki."

On his next pass-by after that, the ferryman remarked, "I know the man. Seminole named Chubb. He's a lieutenant in the Seminole Lighthorse Police."

"What?"

"You didn't know?" He chuckled, then yelled over his shoulder as he pulled to the stern, "They're a tough bunch. Only ten of 'em, but you won't find better fighters in the Nations. With those ten, the Seminoles don't have no trouble keeping the peace in their neck of the woods."

Torn was silent, contemplating this new development. He expected to butt heads with Chubb again. He had no authority in the Nations, though. Now it turned out that John Chubb was the authority.

A couple of pass-bys later, as they drew near the south bank, the talkative ferryman said, "Just last spring I ferried Chubb and two white men over. Thing is, those two white men were as dead as rotten stumps. Belly-down over their saddles, they was. Seems they made the mistake of robbing and killing a Seminole farmer. When a man breaks Seminole law, that's the way he usually winds up."

When they reached the bank, Torn led the grateful mare onto dry land and swung into the saddle. The ferryman wished him good luck. Then he and his taciturn son started the long haul back to the north bank, where the small dogtrot cabin stood in the shade of tall pecan trees.

Torn rode south by east, staying to a trace that looked well-traveled. The ferryman's parting was not simple courtesy or an idle comment. Any lone traveler in the Nations needed all the luck he could get. As federal law did not apply in the Indian Territory, it was naturally a haven for hardcase outlaws of every bent. Good long-rider country, too, with its abundant thickets, rugged hills, and occasional swamp.

The land was generally believed to be inferior to the tallgrass prairie of Kansas for farming or the grazing of large herds of livestock. This was why, Torn reasoned, the government had seen fit to give it to the tribes swept away from their homelands by the relentless westward tide of white expansion.

In most cases, though, the Indians were making the best of a bad situation. Torn saw evidence of this as he neared the town of Mikasuki, along about midday. He saw a scattering of small farms, with more corn than wheat in the fields. The smallest of the Five Civilized Tribes, the Seminoles had rebuilt their tribe on a sound agricultural basis. Torn knew something about cash crops, having been reared on a tidewater plantation. Though tobacco had been a mainstay of the Torn estate, corn had also been grown. It was a sensible crop, less subject to disease and less vulnerable to the vagaries of weather than other grains. A portion could also be used as feed for livestock. Torn saw quite a few cattle and a number of hogs that day on the road to Mikasuki.

The trace topped a ridge thick with hickory, oak, and sumac, and then broke out of the woods and into a valley that was perhaps two miles long and a half-mile wide. The road turned to the east, passing between the forested slope and vast cultivated fields. Elm and willow trees marked the serpentine passage of a creek through the amber fields. Crows called from the woods, and blackbirds darted beneath a handsome blue sky. Straight ahead, at the east end of the small valley, Torn glimpsed ribbons of chimney smoke rising above a cluster of log cabins and chikees. Mikasuki.

The tranquil beauty of the scene both pleased and disturbed him. It would not be easy, he thought, to persuade Mary to leave this peaceful haven behind and risk again the dangers of the tallgrass prairie of Kansas, where, it seemed, Ike Dobson ruled with an iron hand.

He saw several men on horseback coming up the road from the village. Watching them warily, he slowed the mare to a walk. That's when he heard the sound of cantering horses behind him. He twisted around to see two more mounted men closing in on him from behind.

Checking the mare, he waited for them, keeping his hands in plain sight on the saddlehorn.

It came as no surprise to him that one of the riders was John Chubb. Torn noted the conspicuous bruise on the Seminole's hard-set jaw with some satisfaction. While the other men pulled up, Chubb brought his horse right alongside the black mare.

"You in charge of the welcoming committee?" Torn asked, none too friendly.

"You're not welcome here," replied Chubb, coldly.

Torn surveyed the other men. They were a young, tough-looking bunch. They wore the clothes of white men, and the dark, impassive visages of Indian warriors. They fairly bristled with weapons. Each carried a rifle, and at least two pistols, and every one had a knife. Torn figured that they were all Lighthorse Police. Tough, capable, durable fighting men. If worse came to worst, he didn't stand a chance against all five of them.

"I've come to see Mary."

"I'll tell you once. Go away."

Torn met and held Chubb's hostile gaze. It looked like the Lighthorseman wanted nothing more than to pick up right where they had left off in Wichita. And though he didn't really have a valid reason to quarrel with Chubb, Torn wasn't one to back down. It was pride, pure and simple.

"I've always seen things through. I won't change now."

"You're under arrest."

"You can't make an arrest without a warrant issued by all the chiefs of the Seminole Nations."

"So you know the way we do things," said Chubb, a little surprised.

"The law has always interested me."

"It so happens that I have that warrant." A self-satisfied smile lurked at the corners of Chubb's mouth. "I warned Billy Bowlegs that you would come and try to take his granddaughter away against her will."

"That's a lie, and you know it," rasped Torn.

Chubb struck quickly—too fast for Torn, who was braced for trouble, to react. The Seminole's left hand dropped to his Remington, and his right gripped Torn's right hand as Torn reached in reflex for his own sidegun. Before Torn could pull free, Chubb had lifted the Remington out of the cross-draw holster and was swinging it butt-first. Torn broke away, trying to dodge the blow. The pistol butt merely grazed his scalp. He tried to rein the mare away, hoping to put some space between himself and the Lighthorseman, but Chubb lunged out of the saddle with the agility of a panther and carried Torn off the mare. Torn took the brunt of the impact with the hardpacked red clay of the road, and felt the breath squeezed out of his lungs. He grabbed for Chubb, but the Lighthorseman bounced up and out of his reach. Then he grabbed for the Colt Peacemaker—only to freeze when he heard the deadly snicker of a hammer being cocked. Heaving as he tried to get air, he focused on Chubb, who stood in the road with the Remington aimed at him.

"I told you in Wichita I hoped I wouldn't have to kill you," said Chubb flatly. "But I will, before I let you take Mary back."

Torn heard another horse coming fast, felt the vibration in the hardpack upon which he lay. A hot surge of anger pushed him to the brink of recklessness. His hand was wrapped around the butt of the Peacemaker as Mary checked her horse to a sliding stop and jumped to the ground in a thick drift of red dust.

"Stop it!" she yelled, furious. "Stop it, both of you!"

She gave her brother a hard shove and then spun on Torn, standing in the line of fire.

"Clay Torn, you take your hand off that gun right this minute!"

The anger washed away. He was struck by her beauty, and a warm delight just at seeing her again, alive and well, overcame him.

He let go of the Colt. And smiled.

"Mary." It was all he could think to say, and enough for the moment just to speak her name.

Startled by her vehemence, Chubb stood with the Remington down by his side, staring at his sister in shock. The other Lighthorse Police, sensing that the danger of gunplay had passed, looked amused by Mary's pluck and pique.

"You two!" she breathed, thoroughly exasperated. "Always scuffling like . . . like schoolboys."

Torn just gazed, drinking in the sight of her. She wore a simple tribal dress, cream-colored with broad horizontal bands of dark blue edged with the red and yellow sawtooth design favored by the Seminole. Her feet were covered with beaded moccasins, and her long, lustrous black hair was braided, with yellow ribbon tied at the ends of the braids.

She gave him a funny look, happy and dismayed at the same time, and then she came quietly and softly to him, put her arms around him and laid her head against the broad span of his chest.

"Mary!" exclaimed Chubb, aghast.

She stepped away, looking deep into Torn's gray eyes, the furrows of a frown gathering between her brows.

"I am glad you are well."

He saw the fear, and realized that he was the one responsible for bringing it all back to burden her, the nightmare she thought she had finally escaped. The guilt dismayed him, and made him question his motives for coming all this way. Self-doubt was an unfamiliar cross for Clay Torn to bear.

"I need your help, Mary," he said, gruff and resolute.

"I am not free to give it," she admitted, with regret.

"Ike Dobson's stunt back in Wichita turned the townfolk against him. I guess their attitude was that they didn't care what he did as long as he didn't do it in the street and scare the horses. But he scared the horses that night. And the newspaper got into the act. The editor of the Wichita *Eagle* is pro-Granger. He was very interested in the story told him by the son of the Pitchfork Slough station agent. You remember the station agent, don't you, Mary? Ike Dobson had him killed. They shot him down like a dog. Ike's finally gone too far. Now we have a chance to stop him. It won't be easy. But it's the only chance we'll have. Just one shot."

She shook her head, wincing as though the words drove daggers through her.

"I can't. Please, don't ask this of me. I'm finally free of him."

"Are you? I don't think you'll be free until you know for a fact that people like that woman and her child, out there alone in the prairie, can live without fear of Ike and his men."

John Chubb lunged forward, menacing Torn with the Remington, hissing the words through clenched teeth.

"Leave her alone! I'm warning you."

"John, please . . ." began Mary.

"No!" Chubb jammed the barrel of the Remington up under Torn's jaw, forcing his head back. "You're under arrest. Unbuckle your shellbelt and let it drop."

With eyes like cold steel, Torn obeyed. The irrational anger was gone, replaced with an implacable resolve. Now was not the time to settle with John Chubb—not with Mary in their midst. The time would come, though; right or wrong, Torn found himself looking forward to it with grim relish.

Chubb reached under Torn's frock coat with his free hand and drew the saber-knife out of its shoulder rig. A couple of the mounted Lighthorsemen commented on the unique blade in their Muskogee tongue.

"Boy Jim," snapped Chubb. "Ride ahead. Tell Billy Bowlegs that we have the man who came to make trouble."

One of the Lighthorsemen hurrahed his horse into a standing-start gallop down the road toward the distant village.

CHAPTER

26

BILLY BOWLEGS WAS A WIRY OLD MAN, HIS HAIR
streaked liberally with gray, his face like brown leather
with a thousand fine lines. He wore buckskin breeches and
moccasins, and a tribal shirt of bright red and green. There
was nothing about his appearance that indicated an exalted
position as the highly respected town chief. His spry frame
was seated on a log in the shade of a magnificent oak tree,
in front of a chikee, the open-sided, thatch-roofed tradi-
tional dwelling of the Seminole.

The chickee had been shelter enough for the Seminoles
in the almost tropical clime of their Florida homeland, but
it was poor protection from the bitter winter winds which
roared unimpeded across the open plains to pummel the
Oklahoma Territory. And so most families had built log
cabins close by their chikee. The latter, however, remained the preferred dwelling.

As he rode up, escorted by the Lighthorse Police and

Mary, Torn saw several women and a half-dozen children in and around the chikee near which Billy Bowlegs sat. The shelter was cluttered with low, wide tables, which also served as beds, several crates, a split log bench and a couple of barrel chairs. In the center was the star fire— several logs butted together to make a long-burning fire. Everyone was standing still, watching the procession of riders. The Lighthorseman named Boy Jim stood beneath the tree, reins in hand. More people drifted over from other parts of town. There did not seem to be rhyme or reason to the layout of Mikasuki; cabins faced every which way, and there weren't any clearly defined streets.

Billy Bowleg's dwelling stood at the northern rim of town, facing a field of shoulder-high corn. It was this field that had Billy's attention. Busily reloading an old flintlock rifle, he alone exhibited not the slightest interest in the approaching riders. Torn had heard a couple of shots fired as he neared town. He had thought at the time that they must be a signal; now he knew that they had been fired by the chief. As they checked their horses, Billy Bowlegs brought the rifle to his shoulder and fired into the field. Torn looked that way in time to see a blackbird, perched insolently on a cornhusk scarecrow some three hundred feet distant, die in an explosion of feathers. It was damn fine shooting with an old flintlock, and Torn was impressed.

Mary dismounted before the others and hurried to the old chief, giving him a hug and a brief whisper in his ear. Pleasure at this embrace animated the leathery face, and he cast a sly glance at Torn. Mary stepped away to stand respectfully at Billy's shoulder. Bowlegs made a come-closer gesture as Torn stepped down off the black mare, and Torn complied, shadowed by a wary John Chubb, who had Torn's shellbelt and Colt shoulder-slung.

"Damn blackbirds," said Bowlegs over the corncob pipe

gripped in yellowed teeth. "They peel the husk from the ear and eat the kernels. They profit from the fruit of our labors. So Billy makes them pay the price for thievery."

The flintlock braced between his legs, Bowlegs took a paper cartridge from a leather pouch resting on the log beside him, and removed the pipe long enough to bite off the tail end of the wrapping before dropping the cartridge down the barrel. By the shape of the cartridge, Torn knew that the chief was using minié balls, conical slugs that expanded in the barrel when fired. This resulted in a flat trajectory and greater velocity, increasing a rifle's range. And Torn also knew, from firsthand wartime experience, that miniés caused vicious wounds.

Torn made no reply. Bowlegs gave him another sidelong look as he rammed the charge home.

"My grandson says you came as a thief, to steal Billy's granddaughter away from him."

"Your grandson is mistaken. I have not come to take her away against her will. But then, it seems she cannot make her own decisions. She has no will of her own. You have taken it from her."

"Keep a civil tongue in your head," snapped Chubb.

Bowlegs held up a gnarled hand to silence the Lighthorse lieutenant.

"Mary has told Billy about you. How you saved her from Dobson. That you did not have to risk your life to help her, but did anyway. For this, Billy is grateful. Mary and John are like his own children to Billy. They have been in Billy's care since they were little ones, when typhoid took their mother, Billy's own daughter, and her husband."

"So grateful that you issue a warrant for my arrest."

Bowlegs grimaced. "Sometimes we must do what we do not want to do."

"This is what I've hoped your granddaughter would realize."

"She knows. She wants to help you. But she cannot."

"Because you won't let her."

Billy primed the flashpan with black powder from a horn. Pulling the hammer back, the old chief squinted across the field. There weren't any blackbirds at rest on the outstretched "arms" of the scarecrow, but there were a few on the wing. Billy brought the flintlock to his shoulder and fired in one quick, fluid motion. A blackbird plummeted to earth. A prodigious amount of acrid white smoke drifted in Torn's direction.

"Damn blackbirds," Billy said again. "They remind me of white men. They take what does not belong to them. And they are many, as many as the leaves on all the trees in the forest." He set the longrifle against the log and rose to face Torn, arms folded across his chest. "You want to stop Dobson. That's good. Someone has to. But you must do it without our help. We have no reason to help you, and every reason not to."

"He's killing innocent people. Men, women, and children—it makes little difference to him."

Billy sighed. "That is a bad thing. But not uncommon among whites. We know this from personal experience. Our forefathers lived peacefully in Spanish Florida, wanting only to farm our land, and without ill will to anyone. But the white soldiers came first to kill men, women, and children when the slaves of the rich white planters ran away to seek safe haven among us. And then they came again, a little later, because they had seen our land and knew that it was good land and wanted it for their own. Billy himself fought against them, side by side with greater warriors, Osceola and Wildcat. For seven years we made them pay the price for thievery, but in the end they were too many. They took us away in chains, and brought us here.

"But we forgave the white man. Once again we wanted only to work our fields and live in peace. Then the great war among the whites came. Most of us were asked to fight for the government, and we did, for we nurtured no ill will. Again Billy fought, in the Indian Home Guard Regiment. What did we get in return? We were forced to live in refugee camps until we agreed to sell our land for fifteen cents an acre and buy other land for fifty cents an acre. And those of us who fought for the government, we were told that we would get back pay, and bounties for fighting. But we never did. The government said that the records had been lost." Billy shook his head. "We learned our lesson."

Torn surveyed the gathered crowd, the ring of impassive brown faces. He saw no real hostility—with the exception, perhaps, of John Chubb—but neither did he see even a glimmer of sympathy for his cause in the eyes of anyone but Mary.

"I can't defend the government," he admitted. "I fought against it during the war. My family was killed, all our land stolen. But at least in my case the government had reason for treating me that way."

"And yet you are a judge. You represent the government."

"I represent the law. Justice. That's not the government, necessarily. And it was my choice to fight against the government. My choice, and I am to blame for the consequences. Everyone should have that right. To choose the course his life will take. I'm pretty sure that's what I was fighting for. Of all people, you should know that this is something worth fighting for. The government tried to take that freedom from you. Seems to me you're doing the same thing to your granddaughter."

Billy Bowlegs grinned. "You argue good."

"I'm not here to argue. It strikes me, though, that Dobson tried to run Mary's life, and now you're doing the same."

"Don't let him talk to you that way, Grandfather," urged Chubb.

"Be still," ordered Bowlegs. The grin was gone. Now he studied Torn with a thoughtful and quiet dignity.

"The welfare of his people is Billy's responsibility. He does not want to wage war against Dobson. He has learned that in war it does not matter who is right and who is wrong; the outcome belongs to the side that is the strongest."

"You're right in the middle of this war," said Torn. "You just don't know it yet."

For a moment, no one spoke. Billy stared grimly at Torn, and Torn knew there was no need to elaborate on the warning. Billy Bowlegs understood, and the possibilities disturbed him.

Finally, he said, "You are not the enemy, and so you will be made welcome. Stay among us as long as you wish. But when you leave, you will leave alone. It has been decided. It is for the best. Return his weapons to him."

Chubb started to protest, but deemed it wiser to comply, and Torn was reinvested with gun and saber-knife. Bowlegs gave John Chubb some stern advice.

"This man is our guest as long as he chooses to remain. Billy knows now that you were wrong, John. He will not take Mary away against her will. He is a firm believer in free choice."

Bowlegs began to turn away, only to pause and throw a sly glance at Torn.

"Billy hopes, for your sake, that you will not prove him wrong."

"I'm sorry that you came such a long way for nothing."

"I'm not sorry, Mary." Torn struggled briefly with his feelings and the words required to express them. "At least I know that you are safe."

They walked along the creek, surrounded by the cornfields. A good half-mile from Mikasuki. It had been Mary's suggestion. Torn was surprised that there was no chaperoning being conducted by Chubb and the other Lighthorsemen. But then, his horse was back in the village. He wouldn't get far on foot.

It was late in the day. The valley was hot and still. Torn almost longed for the relentless prairie wind. Locusts buzzed in the trees that grew along the run. Something rustled away through the tall cornstalks. A fox, maybe, or a rabbit. The pungent aroma of the rich soil filled his nostrils. Memories distracted him; he could imagine himself a much younger man, blissfully ignorant of the tribulations life would deliver, walking through the fertile fields of the Torn plantation.

"I worried about you," she confessed. "I wanted to go back and find you—just to make sure you hadn't been . . . hurt. But John wouldn't allow it."

There it was again, mused Torn bitterly. John wouldn't allow this, Billy Bowlegs wouldn't allow that. He felt sorry for Mary, and angry at her, too, for not resisting the control of her family in the same way she had finally resisted Ike Dobson's control.

"It doesn't matter," he said.

She heard the dejection that Torn allowed to taint his words, and pulled up short.

"When I married Ike," she said, hoping fervently to

make him understand, "I forsook my family. I went against their wishes. They didn't have to help me when I cried out to them for help. It would be wrong—at the very least, ungrateful—to go against them."

"I know, I know," said Torn, exasperated. Seeing the hurt this curtness brought her, he relented. "It's all right, Mary. Honestly. I really didn't expect you to come back with me."

"I feel as though I owe you that much."

He could see how miserable the dilemma made her. "To be perfectly frank, the real reason I came here was to see you."

Her eyes widened. Her lips parted slightly, as though the revelation took her breath away. Those full, red, desirable lips. He wanted to take her in his arms to kiss those lips, and cursed himself mercilessly.

"Oh, I wish I'd met you years ago," she said. "Before I met Ike. Then things would have turned out so very different."

"I doubt they would have. You see, I'm . . . committed. Just like you."

"To that someone I reminded you of?"

He handed her the daguerreotype. She gazed at it for quite a long time, and Torn could not fathom her expression.

"She's very pretty," said Mary finally. "What's her name?"

"Melony."

"Where is she?"

"I don't know. She disappeared after the war. We were to be wed. I don't even know if she's alive or dead. But until I find out, something inside me won't let go."

She returned the daguerreotype, and as he pocketed it, she stepped in very close and he felt her gentle fingers brush the sore, swollen spot above his right temple, where the butt of Chubb's gun had grazed his scalp.

"It cut the skin," she said solicitously. "You should let me make a poultice of feather moss and mustard root."

Their eyes met and held, and her arms, their skin warm and velvet smooth, circled his neck. He just couldn't fight it any longer. They kissed, a whirlwind of passion sweeping them up.

Mary whispered, "How long can you stay?"

"I'd better leave now."

"The morning is soon enough."

He didn't hear the horses until it was almost too late. He couldn't for one vulnerable moment see anything but Mary, or hear anything but her voice, or feel anything but her body pressed against him and her hot breath against his skin.

His instincts screamed, bringing him crashing back down to earth, and his first thought was that it had to be Chubb, and he resigned himself to the grim fact that he was going to have to deal with Mary's brother after all. But when he looked up and saw the riders coming across the cornfield, and beyond them many more galloping down the road toward Mikasuki, he knew better.

He recognized only one right away. The gambler, Dice Fontane, in that familiar gray claw hammer and white panama. Fontane was one of the four horsemen charging toward them through the tall corn. This time Fontane was brandishing a handgun of considerably larger bore than a hideout derringer. And as Torn threw Mary to the ground and reached for his Colt, Fontane leveled the pistol and fired the first shot.

CHAPTER

27

ONE SHOT WAS ALL THAT TORN ALLOWED THE GAM-
bler. To hit the mark fifty yards away while aboard a
galloping horse required luck or experience, and preferably
both. Fontane didn't have the expertise, and this time luck
deserted him. His shot went wild. Torn's didn't. He drew
the Colt, aimed and fired with cool and unhurried delib-
eration. Arms outflung, Fontane toppled off the horse and
disappeared into the tall corn.

The other three riders started firing, but Torn was already down and out of sight. Mary had scrambled to the
edge of the field and he joined her. Being on foot was no
great disadvantage, Torn figured; he and Mary could conceal themselves while the riders, as long as they remained
mounted, could not.

The corn hid them for a moment from the horsemen.
Bullets clipped the stalks above their heads. Then a horse
came crashing out of the field almost on top of them. The

rider snapped off a shot, straight down, as he went by. Torn fired straight up at him. They both missed. The horse galloped on by and into the creek before the rider could check and turn it. Torn fired again. The bullet smacked into the man's shoulder and carried him out of the saddle. He fell into the creek. The horse shied away from the geyser of water. Torn knew that the shot had not been fatal, and so he was ready when the man came out of the water, hunched over in agony, bringing the six-shooter up slowly, as though it weighed a hundred pounds. Down on one knee, shielding Mary with his body, Torn took careful aim and fired the killing shot. The dead man sprawled flat on his back in the shallows, and ribbons of blood drifted downstream.

"Get back into the corn," Torn told her. "Hide yourself. Stay down and lie still."

Mary crawled deeper into the stand of corn. Torn spun as another horse emerged from the field, scarcely thirty feet away. Torn fired, but the man had quick reactions. Before he died he triggered both barrels of the sawed-off shotgun he was carrying. Torn felt the red-hot sting of double-aught buckshot in his right leg and gasped at the pain as he fell. From mid-thigh to calf he had taken at least a half-dozen pellets. But he counted himself lucky; at closer range he would have taken the whole load.

Crawling, he tried for the cover of the corn. He didn't make it in time. The fourth horseman was bearing down on him. Mary cried out. The rider yanked savagely on the reins, looking behind him, surprised, swinging the gun in his hand. With an empty feeling in his guts, Torn realized that the man had ridden right over Mary. He struggled clumsily to his feet, supporting himself precariously on his uninjured leg, and yelled, hoarse and incoherent. The rider twisted in the saddle.

"You bastard," said Torn through clenched teeth, and fired the Colt's last two rounds.

The man slumped forward and slipped from the saddle, crashing into the corn.

"Mary," breathed Torn, and tried to walk. Putting weight on his right leg sent searing agony lancing through his body. Dizzy, he lost his balance and fell. Cursing this sudden weakness, he let go of the empty Colt and began to crawl, digging his fingers deep into the soil, clawing for purchase, dragging himself inch by painful inch toward the edge of the cornfield.

Then he saw her, coming through the stalks on hands and knees. Seeing him laid out and struggling, she got up and ran the rest of the way, falling to her knees beside him.

"Oh, Clay . . ."

"I'm all right. Stay down."

They could hear a barrage of gunfire from the direction of town. It sounded like a full-fledged battle. In his mind's eye, Torn made a quick count of the riders he had seen galloping down the road toward Mikasuki. At least ten. Maybe more. Not Bar ID men, either. These were new players. He glanced at the man spreadeagled in the creek, and at the other—the one who had carried the greener— now a crumpled heap on the bank. No, these weren't cowboys. They were hardcase riffraff. Men who lived— and died—by the gun. As common as dirt on the frontier. Torn felt rage heat up inside him like a fever. Ike Dobson's hiring of men such as these was the last straw. There would be no mercy in this war now. No quarter.

"Let me look at your leg," said Mary.

"Later."

"There won't be a later for you, Torn."

Mary gasped. Torn's head snapped around.

Dice Fontane stood, swaying slightly, not twenty feet away, at the edge of the cornfield. Blood stained the gray claw hammer coat, high on the right shoulder. He had lost the white panama. But not his gun. This was pointed at Torn.

Torn's eyes flicked to the Peacemaker, a roll and a reach away. It was empty.

"Go ahead. Try it," goaded Fontane. "I told you that nobody messed with Dice Fontane and got away with it. Now I'm dealing the last card. And you lost."

"I shouldn't have tried so hard not to kill you," said Torn flatly.

"Funny thing is, if I'd killed you then, I wouldn't have profited. Now I'll get a thousand dollars on top of the satisfaction. How does it feel, Judge, to be the one with the price on his head?"

"Dobson?"

"That's right. Mr. Dobson put up the reward. Not dead or alive. Just dead."

Torn's mind was racing. His only hope was to keep Fontane talking. At least it was the cardsharp who had the drop on him, and not one of the hired guns. Professionals didn't waste time on idle conversation.

He felt the weight of the saber-knife in its shoulder rig, snug against his side. It wasn't a throwing knife—it didn't have the balance. Somehow he had to draw Fontane closer. Somehow he had to ignore the throbbing pain in his leg when he made his move. Somehow he had to get his hand on the saber-knife. Problem was: Fontane had good reason to remember the saber-knife, and if he had any sense at all he would shoot as soon as Torn made that move.

"So you've been working for Dobson all along."

Fontane grinned. He was enjoying his advantage, wanting to milk it for all it was worth. He wanted to see Torn sweat.

"You shouldn't have made an enemy out of me, Torn. I'm the one told Dobson about you in the first place, when he came to Pitchfork Slough. And I told him where to find you in Wichita. Hell, I would have done all that for nothing. This, too. But it's my lucky day."

"You're a fool. Dobson's fool."

"Oh, no," said Fontane simply. "That's why I brought these men here, instead of to meet up with Dobson, like he wanted. You see, this way, I've got the woman. I always make sure I'm on the winning side of the table. It's just a question now of *which* Dobson I give her to."

"What does that mean?"

"She knows. Don't you, Mrs. Dobson? Drew and Lute want her and Ike out of the way. Nobody's said as much. They don't have to say it. I can tell. It just depends on whether they make their play on the old man real soon. If they do, I'll deliver her to them. What a shame, Mrs. Dobson; if that happens you'll never live to see Kansas. I call it playing both ends against the middle."

"You straddle the fence, you'll likely get cut where it hurts the most," said Torn.

Fontane's derisive laugh degenerated into a coughing fit. Wincing, he grabbed at his shoulder. The gun dropped a fraction. Torn's right hand moved, but Fontane was expecting that, and recovered quickly. He hadn't forgotten the saber-knife, or the feel of its edge against his throat. He took two shuffling steps forward, steadied the gun.

"Go on, Judge. You might as well try. You've got nothing to lose. I'm going to kill you anyway."

CHAPTER 28

FONTANE PULLED THE HAMMER BACK.

"No!" cried Mary, and threw herself across Torn.

"Get out of the way, bitch!" snarled the gambler.

Torn felt her hands groping under his coat. "Mary, no . . ."

Fontane reached down and grabbed her roughly by the arm, trying to peel her off Torn. She came away, unresisting, which caught the cardsharp off balance.

Spinning into him, she drove the saber-knife to the hilt in his belly.

The gambler's mouth gaped open in a soundless scream. His coyote eyes bulged in their sockets. He looked, disbelievingly, into Mary's face, inches from his own, and saw something there that was savage and remorseless and primeval.

"You should watch where you're going," she hissed.

She wrenched ruthlessly downward with the knife and

172

stepped away, extracting the blade. Fontane staggered back two steps, then fell, a gusher of bright blood shooting out of the gaping mortal wound. She had gutted him like a fish. His heels drummed against the ground for a moment, and then the blood came out of his mouth, and he was still, dead eyes staring at the darkening sky.

Struggling to his feet, Torn reached her side and gently took the saber-knife from her hand. The weapon was covered with blood. So were her hand and arm, and more blood had splattered on her dress. As he watched, the savagery faded away, and the Mary he had come to know reappeared. That there was another, darker side to her didn't disturb him. It was there in everyone, sometimes lurking just beneath the surface, sometimes buried deep. There were people like Sergeant Karl Schmidt, who were ruled by the darker side of their nature, and then there were the Mary Dobsons of the world, who took a lot of pushing and prodding before they succumbed.

"I had to do it," she said, her voice hollow. "He was going to kill you."

How strange, he thought, that she felt obliged to apologize.

The distant gunfire was becoming sporadic. It was second nature to him to ride to the sound of the guns. He looked around and saw that all but one of the horses had scattered far out into the cornfields. The exception was the mount of the man with the greener, who stood patiently near the body of its erstwhile rider. Cavalry-trained, judged Torn, a horse inured to gunfire, the survivor of a campaign or two.

Torn started for it, hopping on his good leg and dragging the other, but Mary detained him and handed him the empty Colt Peacemaker.

"Let me," she said. "You'll spook him, coming up on him like that."

Torn doubted that much of anything would spook that horse, but he didn't argue. He wiped the saber-knife on his trousers, sheathed it, and reloaded the Colt while Mary fetched the horse.

A moment later they were mounted double, Mary behind him. Bracing himself against the pain, Torn got the horse into a canter. They followed the creek back to the village.

By the time they got there the shooting had stopped. Torn slowed the horse to a walk, and they passed through a scene of carnage. Acrid gunsmoke tainted the air. In the grim silence of aftershock, the Seminoles milled about. Riderless horses stood still or trotted aimlessly between the cabins. The dead were scattered everywhere. Torn didn't try to take a count. He didn't want to. He'd done enough body counts during the war. But one observation turned his blood to ice. Not all of the Seminole dead were men. There were several women. And one boy who could not have been older than twelve. The hired guns had killed indiscriminately.

"I'm going to kill him, Mary," he muttered, both a warning and an apology in advance.

"I know."

She held onto him a little tighter.

The Seminoles were stoic in their grief. No wailing over the death of loved ones. These, mused Torn, were a people accustomed to tragedy.

Rounding a cabin, they came upon John Chubb standing over the bullet-riddled body of the Lighthorseman, Boy Jim. There were revolvers in Boy Jim's hands. Chubb was reloading his Remingtons. There wasn't a flicker of expression on his face, even when he saw Torn's leg and the blood on his sister.

"Did any get away?" asked Torn.

"I don't know. If so, we'll track them down." He didn't have to tell them what would happen then, and there wasn't the shadow of a doubt that if any of the hired guns had escaped they wouldn't get far. "They came for you, didn't they, sister?"

Mary nodded, too overcome with guilt to speak.

Torn said, "Four split off and made for us. The others were to keep you busy. I think they underestimated the people of this village. They must have been watching from the hills, waiting for the chance."

"We captured one. Billy Bowlegs has him."

They rode on, to the northern outskirts of Mikasuki, where the chief's dwelling was located. A crowd of thirty or forty Seminoles had gathered in a stern circle around the tall oak. Mary slipped off the horse and did her best to assist Torn in a clumsy, offside dismount. The assemblage parted to let them through. Torn wasn't too proud to use Mary for support, and wasted no time in sitting on the log and taking his weight off the leg.

A glimmer of relief appeared on Billy Bowlegs' fierce bronze countenance as he saw that Mary, despite her appearance, was unharmed. He stood, leaning on the old flintlock, a few yards away. Torn wondered how many hired gunmen had fallen as a result of the chief's deadly skill with the longrifle, but deemed it in poor taste to ask.

A white man sat at the other end of the log. He was watching Torn and Mary with keen curiosity. A bandanna tourniquet had been applied to stem the flow of blood from his bullet-shattered knee. But his leggins were soaked with blood, and his boot filled with more, and there was an unhealthy pallor beneath sun-darkened skin and shaggy beard. He was possessed of a calm defiance in the face of certain doom, as he turned his attention back to the old chief.

"So what's it gonna be? You just gonna stand around and watch me bleed plumb to death?"

"Who sent you?" asked Billy. Torn sensed that this wasn't the first time for that query.

"You go to hell."

"Ike Dobson is responsible," said Torn.

"Is that true?" Billy asked the hardcase.

"Does it make any difference? I come here 'cause there was prospects of a big fight. Nothin' I like better. 'Cept maybe a nice young Injun squaw. 'Specially when the chance presents itself to kill red niggers."

Torn smiled bleakly. This attitude was typical of such men. Money was good, but the opportunity to fight was better still. And the gunman was doing his level best to talk himself into a quick execution.

John Chubb pushed through the crowd and strode to Billy Bowlegs.

"Why do you spend words on him when you could spend bullets?"

"We have laws," replied Billy sternly. "He will be held, and brought before the tribal council to answer charges."

Disgusted, Chubb turned away. Billy grabbed him by the arm.

"Remember who you are. Your duty is to uphold our laws. You, most of all, must abide by them."

Chubb wrenched his arm free. He walked over to the prisoner. The man looked him square in the eye, insolently unafraid.

Quick as a rattler's strike, the Lighthorseman cross-drew the Remingtons and fired both simultaneously. The bullets kicked the gunman backward off the log, killing him instantly.

The boom of the Remingtons dwindled across the cornfields.

The silent crowd began to disperse. There was work to do, dead to bury. The sun was setting, drenching the valley in a scarlet light, and it looked to Torn like all the blood spilled this day had come up out of the earth to cover every cabin, every tree, every stalk of corn, and every one of those left among the living. Suddenly, he felt tired. Tired to the bone.

Billy Bowlegs reached Chubb's side, morosely shaking his head.

"This is the law he lived by," said Chubb. "The law of the gun. It is fitting that he die by it."

"For a moment," murmured Billy sadly, "I could not tell the two of you apart."

MARY ASSISTED TORN TO A SMALL ONE-ROOM LOG
cabin at the edge of Mikasuki. Sitting on the cornhusk
mattress that lay across a narrow rope-slat bed, he tore
his trouser leg at the seam and by the light of a tallow
lamp, examined the buckshot wounds both below and
above his knee.

"I'll have to dig out that double-aught," he told her
grimly. "Could you build me a fire?"

She went out to the woodpile and came back with her
arms full. Before long, using kindling from a box in the
corner of the room, she had a nice hot blaze crackling in
the stone fireplace. The warm golden firelight chased the
gathering gloom of night out of the cabin.

"Let me help you," she said as he took the saber-knife
from its shoulder rig.

"Heat the blade. I'll do the rest."

John Chubb entered the cabin, followed by Billy Bow-legs.

Chubb said, "Sister, leave us."

"Stop ordering me around," she snapped. "I'll do what I want. And right now I want to stay right here with Clay."

"You have been among the whites too long," observed Chubb.

"Mary," said Torn, "he's only trying to protect you."

Both Mary and her brother looked at Torn with some surprise. That Torn would take up for Chubb was the last thing either one of them had expected.

"Protect me from what? I am a Seminole woman. I have seen worse wounds. I have treated worse."

"Not the wound. It's me. He just doesn't want you to make another mistake."

Billy Bowlegs crossed the cabin and handed Torn an earthen jug.

"What's this?"

"Choc."

Torn sniffed the potent Indian beer, then set the jug aside. "I'll pass. Thanks all the same."

Billy looked at Mary, who stood defiantly in the middle of the cabin, the saber-knife in hand, looking every bit like she intended to use the weapon on the next person who tried to tell her what to do.

"Granddaughter, he will need a poultice."

"You're just trying to get rid of me," she said, accusingly.

There was a split-log trestle table in the center of the cabin. She drove the point of the saber-knife deep into the top of the table, and stalked indignantly out into the night.

"She is headstrong," remarked Billy, unable to keep the admiration out of his voice.

"You should be proud of her," said Torn. "She wants to do what's right."

Stepping forward, John Chubb drew a knife from the sheath belted at the small of his back. It was another Arkansas Toothpick, similar to the one he had used in that Wichita street-fight with Torn.

"I will help you," said Chubb gruffly. "My hand will be steadier than yours."

Torn hesitated before assenting. He was looking at Chubb, but he could feel Billy watching him closely. The town chief was keenly interested in his response to this unexpected offer from a man who, so far, had been anything but friendly.

Finally, Torn nodded. "Just remember," he said wryly, "it's the leg, not the throat."

John Chubb almost smiled as he turned to the fireplace and knelt to hold the blade in the flames.

Billy bent to recover the jug. Bracing it in the crook of his arm, he took a long drink. Wiping his mouth with a sleeve, he studied Torn soberly.

"You are a brave man, Clay Torn. A good man. You are welcome to stay among us."

"I appreciate the offer, but I'll be leaving at first light."

"You will ride against Ike Dobson alone?"

"Better than waiting for him here. Enough innocent people have died."

Billy gravely nodded and fell silent, lost in thought.

Chubb came over from the fire.

"What are you waiting for?" asked Torn crossly. "Lead poisoning to set in?"

He took a bullet from his shellbelt and bit down hard on it as the Lighthorseman began to probe with the point of the knife for the first buckshot pellet.

* * *

Shortly after the departure of Billy Bowlegs and John Chubb, Mary returned. She carried a bucket of water and a wooden bowl. The latter contained a poultice of feather moss and mustard root. Strips of cloth were draped over one arm. Setting the bowl on the table, she washed the blood from Torn's leg, rinsing the cloth in the water. She did not speak, and Torn was too exhausted to indulge in idle conversation. He was weak, his clothes drenched with a cold sweat. Mary applied the poultice to the buckshot wounds, then dressed the leg with the cloth strips.

Torn began to drift into sleep. The cool touch of her hand on his forehead and the sweet warmth of her breath on his face brought his eyes open. She was leaning over him, her face very close to his. She was smiling, and her eyes were bright.

"Do you know what the name 'Seminole' means? It comes from a Creek word, *se-mi-no-lee*, which means to run away, like a deer. We have always run away from trouble. Not because we were afraid so much, as because we wanted to live in peace. But there are some things you cannot run away from. I am through with running. I will go back with you."

"Does your grandfather know about this?"

"He knows."

"What about your brother?"

"He will do as my grandfather instructs. My grandfather is a chief. The welfare of all the people is his concern. He sees now, after what happened today, that the Seminole cannot run away this time."

Torn drew a deep breath. "Mary, I don't want you to come back with me. It's too dangerous."

"But isn't that why you came here?"

"You know why I came."

She stood, went to the door and closed it. The tallow

lamp was still burning on the table. She blew it out. Returning to the bed, she bent down to kiss him, a bold and passionate kiss. Her fingers worked at the buttons of his shirt with a feverish haste.

"Mary, listen..."

"We'll talk about it in the morning," she whispered, and kissed him again.

But in the morning, when Torn awoke, Mary was not there to talk to. He stood, tentatively testing his leg. To his surprise, there was very little pain. The poultice had done its job. Torn was glad of that. During the war he had seen many men lose arms or legs due to gangrene or blood poisoning. One of the most ghastly and enduring memories was the stack of amputated limbs always seen outside field hospitals.

The leg would heal. That was about all that Torn could find in the way of good news this morning. He had an odd and pervasive sense of guilt when he thought about Mary, and what had happened between them last night. She was, after all, a married woman, no matter how bad a character Ike Dobson was. Torn was unhappy with himself for giving in to desire. It spoiled the moment for him.

He found his trousers, neatly repaired by someone who was a top hand with needle and thread. Mary again. Torn quickly dressed and armed himself, and grimly stepped out into the morning light. It was time to make a quick exit from Mikasuki.

Emerging from the little cabin, he pulled up short, confronted by a ring of riders.

There was John Chubb, with four other Lighthorsemen, three of whom Torn recognized as members of the welcoming committee that had met him upon his arrival yesterday. The young, solemn Seminole warriors were armed to the teeth. The sixth person was Mary. She was clad in buckskin leggins and moccasins, and wearing a man's flannel shirt that was entirely too large for her. Still, the attire could not quite conceal the very womanly figure that Torn had become so intimately familiar with the night before.

Mary had the reins of Torn's black mare in hand, and she kicked her own mount forward to deliver the leathers to him. She smiled down at him, the warm and knowing and secret smile of lovers everywhere. Torn forced himself to return it, then quickly looked away. He gave Chubb a wary study. But whatever John Chubb knew, or felt, remained hidden behind a countenance that was as animated as stone.

"So, what's this all about?" asked Torn.

"We ride with you," said Chubb.

"I didn't think you wanted to get involved in the white man's problems."

"We didn't want to. We are forced to." Chubb glanced at his sister with grim resolve. "If Ike Dobson wants a fight, then he'll have one."

Torn swung stiffly into the saddle. "We're outnumbered," he advised Chubb. "Dobson will have fifteen, twenty men. Maybe more."

Chubb's faint smile was ice cold. He looked at the other four Lighthorsemen, and said, "Good. Then it will be a fair fight."

CHAPTER

30

A MILE FROM THE NORTH FORK OF THE CANADIAN, the Lighthorseman whom John Chubb had sent ahead to scout Groame's Crossing returned to give his report. This he did in his native tongue, and while Torn waited patiently for the translation, he did not have to understand the words to perceive that all was not well.

"Something's wrong," Chubb told him. "There is an old ship's bell on a post on this side of the river. Samuel rang the bell to summon the ferry. He could see smoke coming from the chimney of the ferryman's cabin. But no one came out of the cabin when he rang the bell. He saw no one at all."

Torn was silent for more than a minute, looking in the direction of the river, frowning in thought.

Finally, Mary could wait no longer. She remembered how, on the train, Torn had figured out that Ike would use the telegraph to order his men waiting at the station up-line, to stop the westbound. She recalled that he had guessed that Dobson would remount his men on the cavalry horses to continue his pursuit across the tallgrass prairie. And she remembered Torn warning them, in the crib on the Wichita line, that Dobson was closing in, only minutes before the attack came. Somehow, Clay Torn had stayed one step ahead of Ike Dobson. She didn't know how he had done it, but she sensed that he was doing it again.

"What do you think?" she asked him.

"I think the wrong man rang that bell," he replied. "I think that if I go give it a try, something will happen."

"I'll go with you," said Mary.

"We'll all go," said Chubb.

"No. We'll wait an hour, and then I'll go alone. The rest of you stay hidden in the brush along the bank where you can see but not be seen. If the ferryman comes for me, I'll cross alone. That way we'll find out what's going on over on the other side."

"If Ike's over there, he'll kill you," said Mary.

"Maybe," said Torn coldly, not looking at her. "Maybe I'll kill him. If I do, it'll be over. You can go home and live with your people in peace."

"Clay . . ." Her tone was anguished.

Torn fastened bleak gray eyes on John Chubb. He didn't have to say what was on his mind. The Lighthorseman gave his answer in a curt nod. He would keep his sister out of harm's way. Torn knew that he could rely on Chubb for that much, if nothing else.

They moved off the road, into the cover of a grove of cedar interspersed with sumac. Dismounting, they loosened saddle cinches, then searched out shade. It was late morning, hot and still, without a breath of wind. Thunderclouds were anchored in the bright blue sea of heaven.

Cicadas droned in the brush. Cardinals flickered through the cedar.

No one spoke. Sitting with his back to a boulder, Torn watched the Lighthorsemen, sitting cross-legged within reach of their horses, checking their weapons with methodical care. Torn figured they all sensed, as did he, that there was a fight ahead of them. This was a time not for idle talk, but rather for quiet solitude. A time to think of loved ones. A time to make peace with one's self. It was a time that Torn knew well, that he had shared with fellow soldiers on the eve of a dozen major battles during the war.

For a while Mary sat in silence near her brother, looking nervous and unhappy. Eventually, as Torn expected, she came to him.

"Waiting is so hard," she said.

"You had a rough time on the train, as I recall," he replied, and smiled. "Waiting for us to pull out of Pitchfork Slough."

The smile encouraged her to plead her case once more. "Please, Clay. Let me go with you."

He shook his head.

"I don't want you to die. I don't... want to lose you," she said.

"Mary..." He had trouble putting it into words, so he took the daguerreotype from the inside pocket of his frock coat.

"I know," she said, disconsolate. "You can't lose what you never had. But maybe someday..."

"Maybe someday," he agreed, though he knew that those somedays never came to pass.

A while later, Torn rose, tightened the cinch on the black mare, and stepped into the saddle. John Chubb came forward.

"We'll be there."

Torn nodded curtly, rode back down the road, and turned toward Groame's Crossing.

Near where the cable was attached to a piling on the south bank was a large brass ship's bell hanging from a crosspiece attached to a pair of pole uprights. Torn rang the bell while still mounted, and peered across the wide, fast-moving river, watching the dogtrot cabin beneath the tall pecans on the far bank. A couple of hawks soared overhead, and for a moment they were the only living things Torn could see. He rang the bell again. Then he heard the call of a whippoorwill. He knew immediately that it wasn't a whippoorwill at all, but a signal made by someone concealed in the brush across the river. It was all that he needed by way of confirmation that something was amiss here. Whippoorwills did not sing with hawks in the vicinity.

Someone emerged from the dogtrot. Torn was pretty sure that it was the ferryman. He descended the bank to the moored ferry, followed by his brawny son. In minutes they had the ferry started across the river. Torn ceaselessly scanned the far bank. Everything *looked* normal.

Drawing near, the ferryman called out a howdy that sounded right enough. Torn did not reply, and dismounted. The ferry ran up on the sand and gravel of the shallows. The ferryman's son ran out the boarding planks. Torn led the mare aboard, and noticed that the ferryman was looking past him, as though he expected Torn to have company.

"I remember you," said the ferryman. "You was the one lookin' for the two Seminoles. Hope you don't mind my asking, but did you find 'em?"

"You running a ferry?" asked Torn, tense, "or a newspaper?"

"Just wondering. No offense." He nodded to his son. The latter was about to pull in the gangplank when the sound of hoofbeats spun Torn around. Much to his dismay, he saw Mary galloping out of the screen of willows and deadfall that covered the south bank. John Chubb was just a jump behind her. Torn swore under his breath. He could guess what had happened. Mary had waited for the right moment, and then made a break for it. She was bound and determined to cross the river with Torn. And her brother was trying to stop her.

The snicker of a gunhammer pulled Torn's attention back to the ferryman. A Colt Navy .36 was in the ferryman's ham-sized fist now. Torn had scanned them both for weapons, and he had no idea where the pistol had been concealed. Not that it much mattered at this point.

"Don't try . . ." started the ferryman.

But Torn threw caution to the wind. "Mary!" he yelled. "It's a trap! Get back!"

The ferryman laid the barrel of the Navy Colt across Torn's scalp. Torn went down on hands and knees, fighting to stay conscious.

Mary was almost to the river's edge when she checked her horse into a sliding stop. A few lengths behind her, John Chubb did the same.

"Grab the woman!" hollered the ferryman. His son looked scared and confused. Nonetheless, he leaped from the ferry, lumbered through the shallows and reached Mary before she could turn the horse. Big, muscle-sheathed arms reached up to encircle her waist and dragged her, struggling vainly, from the saddle. Beyond, Chubb drew one of his Remingtons. But he didn't fire. He didn't have a clear shot. The boy backed up through the shallows, keeping Mary between him and the Lighthorseman. Mary was fighting like a wildcat, but she couldn't break free. The ferryman stepped forward, grabbed Mary's arm and wrenched her up onto the ferry. He pulled her close and put the gun to her head, watching Chubb.

"Back off, or I'll kill her!" yelled the ferryman.

"Shoot him!" snapped Torn, still groggy, and striving clumsily to regain his equilibrium and get to his feet. "He won't do it!"

But John Chubb remained unconvinced. Holstering the Remington, he raised both hands away from his sides, gripping the pivoting horse with his knees.

"Boy," said the ferryman, "get shed of that mare and take his gun."

The son gave the mare a rump slap that sent the horse splashing into the shallows and crow-hopping back to the bank. When he got in close to Torn, the latter rose up and threw a punch. The son took it on the shoulder, then threw one of his own that doubled Torn over. Torn felt the weight of the Colt Peacemaker removed. He stayed down on one knee, looked up at the ferryman through a haze of pain and reckless anger. He hugged himself, acting like the blow had hurt him more than it actually had, wanting to keep his arms in tight. For it occurred to him that they didn't know about the saber-knife, concealed under his coat in the shoulder rig, and he wanted to keep it that way.

"Start haulin' us across," ordered the ferryman, and his son obediently went to the couple cable. The ferry lurched as the boy pulled for all he was worth. Torn could testify that the young man was as strong as an ox.

Mary stopped struggling. She was watching Torn. The ferryman split his attention between Torn and Chubb, keeping the Colt Navy pressed against the side of her head.

The main current of the river caught the ferry and pushed it down the curve of the cable. The first half of the crossing was the easy part, and the ferryman knew that his son needed no assistance until time came for the long hard pull up the far side of the curve to the opposite bank.

"I had to do it," he told Torn, gruffly apologetic. "They got my woman under the gun in the cabin yonder. Said if I didn't bring you across they'd kill her."

"They would, too," said Torn.

The ferryman nodded. "That was plain to see."

Torn turned his gaze to the north bank. A passel of men had emerged from the cabin. More appeared from the brush. Most of them were carrying rifles. Torn thought he could make out Ike Dobson among the men in the shadow of the dogtrot.

"They came at dawn," explained the ferryman. "One of 'em kept talking about a big fight in Mikasuki. Said he'd escaped. The others look like cowboys. That one didn't. He looked like a gunslinger. Big man name of Dobson said they'd wait here a day or two. Figured you'd be coming this way. This is the obvious place to cross for someone coming north out of the Seminole Nation. At first I told 'em that I wouldn't help. They got killin' in their eyes. But then they put my wife under the gun..."

Already they were almost halfway across the river. Torn knew he had to act, and act fast. But for the fact that Mary had invited herself along, he would have permitted the ferryman to deliver him to Dobson, and he would have taken his best shot at the Bar ID boss. But there was no way he would allow Ike to get his hands on Mary again. No way.

His instincts had been right on the money again. They had told him that Dobson and his men were here. It made sense that Dobson wouldn't let the ferryman respond to the summons of the Lighthorseman named Samuel. That might have sprung the trap. And it made sense that Dobson would think twice about attacking Mikasuki. After all, a passel of hired killers had failed in just such an assault. Ike was crazy, but not suicidal. Better to wait and see if Torn would bring Mary to him.

Again, Torn listened carefully to his instincts. An innocent woman's life hung in the balance.

They had reached the bottom of the taut cable's curve, dead center in the Canadian. The ferryman's son began to grunt at the exertion as he heaved on the cable, literally trying to pull the ferry against the current. Torn knew that the ferryman would have to lend a hand.

"You go sit next to him," the ferryman told Mary. "Don't make trouble. Don't try to swim for it. The current is strong; the river's wide. You'll drown for sure."

"I'd rather drown," said Mary defiantly.

"Do as he says," snapped Torn.

"All right," Mary said. She put her faith, and her life, in Torn's hands once more.

The ferryman let her go. She crossed to Torn, and got down on her knees beside him. The ferryman nodded his satisfaction with the arrangements, snugged the Colt Navy under his belt, and turned to give his son an assist. Torn gestured for Mary to stay down with one hand as he slipped the other under his coat. He waited until the ferryman was at one end of the ferry and the son was at the other. Then he made his move.

The young man cried out a warning—a cry sharply curtailed by the caress of razor-sharp steel at his throat. The ferryman spun, filling his hand with the pistol, but it was too late to risk a shot. The young man started to give Torn trouble. Torn knew he was no match for someone whose muscles had been honed by years of river crossing. So he used the saber-knife, pressing just enough to break the boy's skin. A rivulet of bright red blood trickled down his throat.

The ferryman didn't know what to do. He was caught

between a rock and a hard place. If it went one way he lost his wife. If the other, he lost his son. He swung the Colt Navy in Mary's direction, thinking stand-off. But Torn had stilled the son, and now reached down to remove his Colt from the boy's belt. Thumbing the hammer back, he aimed the Peacemaker at the ferryman.

"Don't even think about it," he rasped. "I'll kill you where you stand. Drop the gun."

"I can't." The ferryman's voice was hollow with despair.

"They won't kill your wife."

"You don't know that!" yelled the other.

"I know my enemy," replied Torn confidently.

But the ferryman wouldn't drop the gun, and Torn had a split second to agonize over his own choices. If it came down to it, could he kill this man?

He didn't have to make the choice.

Dobson and the Bar ID men started shooting from the north bank.

CHAPTER 31

THERE WERE TEN OF THEM, MAYBE A DOZEN. TORN didn't have the leisure to count. All of them began to fire at the ferry. Hot lead burned the air all around Torn and the others. The ferryman pivoted into a bullet and went down, dropping the Colt Navy. His son uttered a strangled cry and began again to struggle against Torn's hold, now mindless of the blade at his throat. Torn let him go. The boy took a couple of steps toward his father, and stepped into a hail of lead.

Torn wasn't shocked or surprised by this gundown. He had seen too much of Dobson's handiwork lately to be surprised. Ike had seen that events on the ferry were turning against him, and he had responded in the only manner he knew.

What bothered Torn was that they were sitting ducks. The ferry was suspended on the cable in the middle of the river. He could think of only one desperate way to solve the problem. Holding the Peacemaker scant inches from the arm-thick cable, he fired three rounds in quick succession.

The cable frayed, unraveled, and came apart with a sound not unlike a gunshot. The current caught the ferry and shoved it downstream with such violence that Torn lost his balance and fell. He tried to get up, felt the ferry rock one way and then the other under his feet, and then fell again as a wave of river water crashed over the side and drenched him. He saw Mary sliding past him on the slick planking; lashing out, he caught her arm and kept her from being washed overboard. A glance told him that the bodies of the ferryman and his son were gone. He could only hope they were already dead; if not, and only wounded, they would surely drown.

The ferry pitched and bucked and pivoted like a spirited bronco. Belly-down, legs splayed, Torn realized that he had lost the Colt Peacemaker. He had Mary in one hand and the saber-knife in the other. Driving the point of the saber-knife as hard as he could into the planking, he held on for dear life, as the ferry dipped into a swell and more water engulfed them. Dimly, over the roar of the river, he could hear a fierce exchange of gunfire. Gunfire, he decided, was the least of his worries right now.

With a terrific jolt that almost dislodged them, the ferry suddenly slowed. Torn seized the opportunity to lift his head and take a look around. The current had thrown the ferry against a sandbar, and the ferry had been deflected out of the main channel and into a narrow backwater between the sandbar and the bank. The ferry turned slowly in the still shallows. Torn was quick to realize that they had been driven near the north bank of the river. That was definitely the wrong bank as far as he was concerned, for this was the side owned by Ike Dobson and his Bar ID boys.

There was heavy gunfire from upstream. The Lighthorsemen on one bank and the cowboys on the other were shooting at each other on the run; both groups were still chasing the runaway ferry. In the minutes since Torn had shot the cable apart and set the ferry adrift, the Canadian's current had carried the craft downstream faster than horses could gallop. But Torn knew that there was no time to waste. He and Mary had to find cover.

He slid off the ferry and into water that was waist-deep, holding out a hand to Mary. Together, they waded ashore. Torn could hear horses crashing through the brush, could feel the beat of their hooves beneath his feet. The gunfire was drawing closer. A man cried out in pain, somewhere close on this side of the river. Chalk one up for the Seminole Lighthorsemen, thought Torn.

He set a course for a nearby thicket of willows, limping on his bad leg, acutely aware of their predicament. His only weapon was the saber-knife, gripped in his right hand. His allies, the Lighthorsemen, were across the Canadian, and they were going to stay there. The river was too swift to cross at this point.

They reached the willows just as a rider broke into sight.

It was Ike Dobson.

Dobson was shooting across the river. He galloped past Torn and Mary, laying low in the brush, only to check his horse sharply and look at the ferry trapped in the backwater, then down at the sandy bank. Torn cursed silently. Even as Dobson's head swiveled toward the willows, Torn was gathering himself up for the charge.

"Clay . . . !"

He broke free of her, his features savage and resolute. "Stay down, Mary."

He came crashing out of the brush, clumsy on his game leg, as Dobson spun his horse around. Torn launched his jump off his good leg. Dobson fired at point-blank range, but Torn was already dragging him out of the saddle, and Torn felt the bullet snag his frock coat, graze the shoulder rig of the saber-knife, and miss him by a flea's hair.

Even as he fell Dobson managed to hook his brawny arm around Torn's neck, carrying Torn down with him. They rolled into the shallows, locked in hand-to-hand combat. When they stopped rolling, Dobson was on top, trying to point the barrel of his sidegun at Torn's face. Torn was striving to turn the gun away with his left hand and drive the saber-knife into his adversary with his right. But Dobson had a good grip on Torn's right wrist. It was a contest of sheer brute strength, and neither man gave an inch.

Snarling from exertion through gritted teeth, Dobson said, "I'm going to kill you, you bastard, if it's the last thing I do."

Torn heard the rifle shot just as the impact of the bullet kicked Dobson's body sideways and off of him. Torn rolled away. For a fraction of a second he was confused, by reflex glancing across the river. His first thought was that one of the Lighthorsemen had done the deed. His next thought was that the shot had come from *this* side of the river; the impact had thrown Dobson deeper into the shallows. Torn heard the rustle of brush and spun to see Mary running toward him.

"Get down!" he yelled. He wanted to turn toward Dobson, to find Dobson's gun. Instead, he got up and lunged at Mary, bringing her down into the sand as, out of an eye-corner, he saw movement in the willows, the flash of sunlight off a gunbarrel.

Two men, on foot, stepped out into the open.

Torn thought he recognized one from the fight on the

westbound train. This one looked pale and haggard, his eyes dazed, like a man suffering from a long illness. The other one had a funny half-smile; a lazy, insolent, cruel kind of smile. The first man carried a pistol, the other a repeating rifle. Somehow Torn knew that this was the rifle that had just fired.

"Howdy, mamma," sneered the one with the rifle.

There wasn't an ounce of respect in the greeting. Suddenly Torn realized who these men were.

Lute looked at Torn, then glanced at the body of Ike Dobson lying faceup in the shallows.

"Well damn. Looks like I shot the wrong man. Accidental-like."

Dobson's sons, thought Torn. Drew and Lute. He didn't know which was which, and didn't care. He remembered what Ted Judah had said, back at the Lady Gay in Wichita.

Word has it that they don't much care for their stepmother. That they'd sooner see her dead than back home . . .

And there was no doubt in Torn's mind that they had meant to murder their father.

"You two better say your so-longs," smiled Lute as he worked the rifle's lever action to jack another round into the breech. "'Cause this is as far as you go."

Torn measured the distance, and knew with certainty that it was too much ground to cover. He wouldn't reach them in time. He would surely die.

But that wasn't going to stop him.

The barrel of the rifle swung toward him.

Torn lunged.

A rifle spoke. But it wasn't Lute's rifle. The bullet turned Lute halfway around. He took one step, then collapsed. Drew, stunned, and reacting too slowly, was distracted by this unexpected turn of events. Too late, he realized that Torn was coming at him hard. He brought the sidegun up. Torn knocked it aside and struck with the saber-knife, still running flat out. They fell. Torn rolled away, leaving the saber-knife imbedded to the hilt in Drew's chest.

"Clay!" It was Mary, shouting a warning.

Torn had already seen Lute getting up. This Dobson was too mean for one bullet to kill. Torn lunged for Drew's pistol. Staggering, Lute swung the rifle around. They fired simultaneously.

Torn stood up slowly, stepped through the shredding gunsmoke to Lute Dobson's side. Lute breathed one last shuddering breath, and was gone.

He went to Mary, who had waded into the shallows and knelt beside Ike Dobson. Ike was still alive, but barely.

"My own son . . . backshot me . . . taught 'em well . . . didn't I, Mary?"

Bloody froth drooled from the corners of his mouth with every word. The bullet had ripped through his lungs. He was drowning in his own blood.

Watching Ike Dobson struggle for his last breath, it occurred to Torn that there were a lot of Kansas homesteaders who were bound to breathe a lot easier from now on.

He lifted his gaze to the far bank and saw a lone horseman.

John Chubb lifted his rifle over his head. Torn figured that Chubb had fired the shot that had wounded Lute. The shot that had given Torn a fighting chance against the Dobson brothers. Funny how things worked out.

Suddenly, Chubb swept the rifle down, stock to shoulder, and aimed it at them.

No, not at them. Torn whirled as a half-dozen riders walked their horses through the willows.

They pulled up in a half-circle, guns in hand. Six dusty, haggard, grim hombres. They spent a moment looking at the Dobsons, at Mary, at Torn, at the Lighthorsemen across the river. They did not speak. And they did not open fire.

"I reckon it's finished," said one. "All the Dobsons are dead."

"Not all," said Torn. "There's one left."

Mary stood up, staring at Torn. The spokesman for the Bar ID bunch looked curiously at her. He knew, as did Mary, what Torn meant, and he turned this new thought over in his mind.

The cowboy holstered his sidegun, touched his hat to Mary, and reined his horse around. The others followed suit. They drifted back into the brush and disappeared from sight.

"What are you saying?" asked Mary, incredulous. "It's over, and I must go back to live with my people."

"Must you? You were Ike Dobson's wife. Now you're his widow. Seems to me that the Bar ID is yours now."

"I'm a Seminole," she said slowly, enunciating each word carefully, as though she were trying to make herself understood to someone who couldn't quite grasp what was going on. "There are a lot of people in Kansas who wouldn't sit still for an Indian woman inheriting a ranch. In fact, aren't there laws against that?"

"I'm a judge. I'll just change the law."

She shook her head in amazement. "You never give up, do you?"

"No. Never. How about you?"

She took a deep breath. "I guess not. You wouldn't let me, anyway, would you?"

Torn smiled. "This war's over. Let's go start another one."

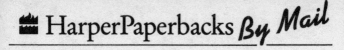